"You want me to be your love slave for the week?" Mitch asked

"It would get this mutual attraction out of our systems," Nicole admitted. Then an impish smile crossed her face. "Besides, I thought the love slave part would be kind of fun."

Mitch laughed. "Keeps you in charge, doesn't it?"

She shrugged, neither admitting nor denying his claim. "Do you have a better idea?"

Leaning forward in his chair, Mitch reached out and touched her thigh with two fingers, slowly drawing a pattern on her slick skin down to the inside of her knee. Judging from the quick catch of Nicole's breath and the darkening of her eyes, he knew she liked it. Mitch couldn't deny that he thoroughly enjoyed arousing Nicole's senses, and he had to admit he liked her completely and totally aware of him. As she was right now.

"I think there should be no restrictions on either one of us," he said finally, sitting up and bracing his hands on his knees. "I'll be your love slave and do anything you ask—as long as you'll agree to do the same for me."

When it seemed as if she was about to argue, he put his finger over her lips, silencing her. "After all, Nicole," he said, giving her a heated look, "I have a few fantasies of my own I'd like to fulfill...."

Dear Reader,

I hope you've enjoyed all the books in the FANTASIES INC. miniseries. This last book, *Wild Fantasy*, more than lives up to its title and is everything a fantasy should be—sexy, erotic and a little bit forbidden. Mitch Lassiter and Nicole Britton have secretly wanted each other for years. Now, partnered for a week-long charity event on a lush island resort brimming with wicked possibilities, they make a pact to indulge in a hot, steamy, anything-goes affair. Trouble is, neither one of them anticipates just where their wildest fantasies will lead them....

Speaking of wild, hot and erotic...be sure to look for my next release in Harlequin's newest—and hottest—series yet: Harlequin Blaze! *Heat Waves* will hit the shelves in October 2001.

I'd love to hear from you. You can write to me at P.O. Box 1102, Rialto, CA 92377-1102, or e-mail me at janelle@janelledenison.com. For a list of my upcoming releases, check out my Web site at www.janelledenison.com.

May your wildest reading fantasies come true.

Janelle Denison

Books by Janelle Denison

HARLEQUIN TEMPTATION
679—PRIVATE PLEASURES
682—PRIVATE FANTASIES
732—FORBIDDEN
759—CHRISTMAS FANTASY
799—TEMPTED
811—SEDUCED
832—SEDUCTIVE FANTASY

WILD FANTASY
Janelle Denison

HARLEQUIN®

TORONTO • NEW YORK • LONDON
AMSTERDAM • PARIS • SYDNEY • HAMBURG
STOCKHOLM • ATHENS • TOKYO • MILAN • MADRID
PRAGUE • WARSAW • BUDAPEST • AUCKLAND

A special thank-you to Carly Phillips and Julie Kenner, for
sharing in the fantasy and for making the project so much fun.

A heartfelt thank-you to my editor, Brenda Chin,
whose unending enthusiasm, encouragement and belief
makes each book I write a reality.

And to Don, who fulfills my wildest fantasies. I love you.

ISBN 0-373-25944-1

WILD FANTASY

Copyright © 2001 by Janelle Denison.

Prologue

"HERE'S THE AD you wanted to proof for the annual charity event on Wild Fantasy."

Merrilee Schaefer-Winston smiled at her assistant as she retrieved the copy of the advertisement. She just needed to give it a quick glance over before she sent it out to newspapers and travel agents throughout the country. "Wonderful. Thank you, Danielle."

The young girl's eyes sparkled enthusiastically. "If previous years are anything to go by, this event should be a smashing success—for the guests *and* the charities that win."

Merrilee nodded, feeling equally optimistic. "That's what I'm hoping."

Danielle left the office to return to other duties and Merrilee leaned back in her chair, scanning the information and the bold caption blazoned across the top of the ad: Wild Fantasy. Where Anything Goes And Anything Is Possible.

Including love, Merrilee thought. Yes, especially that.

Three years ago, she realized she had more money than she knew what to do with as a result of the phenomenal success of her fantasy resorts and the money her late husband had left her. Consequently, Merrilee decided to try something different on one of her island resorts: a vacation that would not only benefit her guests, but other people's lives as well. Thus, the idea of

a charity event was born. Out of the four island geta-
ways she owned, Wild Fantasy seemed the perfect
place to host the kind of games that would be just as uninhibited as the island's name implied.

Her rules were simple and straightforward. Single
guests paired up for a week to engage in sexy, adventurous games with the goal of accumulating points and
ultimately winning monetary prizes for a chosen charity. While the main object was to have fun and interact
with your partner, with each successive competition the
challenges grew more intense and difficult, requiring
both partners to work together to achieve goals or be
eliminated from the contest.

In the process of striving to win, most people discovered things about themselves they never knew they
possessed. Physical strengths they'd never tapped into
before, and the internal fortitude to overcome emotional weaknesses and vulnerabilities.

Merrilee's greatest hope was that everyone left the island with a new respect for their own individual abilities, and a sense of pride for what they accomplished in
their quest to win. On a more personal level, her fondest
wish was that her guests made a more intimate connection with their partner. Sometimes love happened during the course of fun and games, and other times the
couple parted as friends. Either way, everyone was
guaranteed a good time, along with a personal fantasy
request of their own to be fulfilled during their stay.

Merrilee had received many letters from her guests
about the Wild Fantasy Charity Event she hosted,
thanking her for not only her generosity in helping various charities, but for bringing someone special into
their lives. Soul mates had met and fallen in love with a
little direction and guidance provided by the event.

Merrilee sighed, knowing exactly how it felt to connect with someone who was intrinsically part of your soul. For her, that person had been Charlie Miller, a man who'd captured her heart, then died in the Vietnam war before they could begin a life together. The personal loss had left her empty deep inside, the kind of devastating void not even her marriage to Oliver Weston had been able to fill.

Recollections of Charlie Miller prompted thoughts of C. J. Miller, the new, evasive employee who'd been hired on as Fantasies, Inc.'s commuter pilot. There was something about the man that kindled a warmth and the kind of forbidden desire she hadn't experienced in too many years to count. Absently, she fingered the heart-shaped ruby necklace she wore, a gift from an "admirer" whose identity remained elusive—just as elusive as C. J. Miller.

Wild Fantasy. Where anything goes and anything is possible.

The phrase echoed in Merrilee's mind and called upon a fantasy or two of her own. Maybe it was time for *her* to see what was possible, and discover who, exactly, C. J. Miller was.

Feeling a spark of excitement, she approved the ad copy, then attached a note to Danielle and let the words she wrote be her guide as well.

Let the Wild Fantasy begin.

1

HE'D RECOGNIZE that thick tumble of honey-blond hair and incredible body made for sin anywhere.

Eyes riveted to the enticing sight, Mitch Lassiter watched the long-legged beauty follow the hostess across the crowded dining area of the country club where he was waiting for his mother to arrive for their lunch date. Dressed in a coral-colored cotton tank dress that accentuated her golden summer tan and enhanced her lush, toned figure, she effortlessly captured the attention of every red-blooded male in the near vicinity.

Her stride was confident, the sway of her hips inherently graceful. An affable smile tilted her lips as she connected with various appreciative gazes. Yet for all her outward friendliness and warmth, there was something elusive about her that kept Mitch guessing about the real woman beneath the easygoing, independent facade.

Nicole Britton. Bold and spirited, wild and impetuous, and sexy as hell with a competitive streak a mile wide. He'd known her for the past seven years, ever since their mothers had become good friends and had discovered her competitive nature a few years ago at a family get-together when she'd invited him to play a game of pool. Winning had been her sole focus. Assertive and controlled during her shots, yet tempting and teasing him with her overtly flirtatious behavior during *his*, she'd claimed victory...three times in a row.

Despite losing, the evening had been one of the most enjoyable he could recall in recent memory. His Executive Fleet Auto Sales business and family obligations had consumed his life since his father's death, leaving little time to indulge in fun, or even a relationship with a woman. But that night he'd nearly given into the undeniable attraction between them and asked her out on a date, until he'd caught their mothers watching them with a little too much interest. He knew what a mistake it would be to give either one of their parents any reason to hope or believe their involvement would lead to something serious and lasting.

At the time, Mitch hadn't been looking for anything binding or long-term, and judging by Nicole's carefree, noncommittal attitude since her breakup with an up-and-coming city councilman about a year before, he was fairly positive she felt the same. In a split second he considered the possible strain to their mothers' friendship if things didn't work out between him and Nicole. He also considered the unwanted pressure and expectations that might be placed on either of them if they were to become involved. With these factors in mind, he had resolved to keep things between them casual, amicable and uncomplicated the whole way around.

But that decision hadn't stopped him from wanting her. And it certainly hadn't curbed Nicole's inclination to tease and flirt with him when they were together, which only served to build and heighten the sexual tension between them.

He shook those thoughts from his mind just as Nicole turned her head in his direction, causing her silky, shoulder-length hair to ripple with shimmering highlights. Vibrant green eyes searched the area and came to an abrupt stop on him seconds before the hostess halted beside his table.

Surprise lit her gaze and a slow, beguiling smile curved her mouth. "Fancy meeting you here, Mitchell," she drawled, her tone infused with familiar sass.

He inclined his head in greeting and smiled easily in return, feeling that beginning tingle of sexual chemistry the two of them generated whenever they were near each other. "It's nice to see you again, Nicole."

Very nice, indeed. Up close, she not only looked spectacular and incredibly sexy, but smelled soft and feminine, with a hint of warm, ripe apricot—an intoxicating, alluring combination that clenched his stomach muscles with heated awareness.

With effort, he shifted his gaze back to the hostess. "I'm here to have lunch with my mother, Heather. I think you've directed Ms. Britton to the wrong table."

"Oh, no, Mr. Lassiter." The young girl shook her head emphatically and placed another menu on the table. "Your mother and Mrs. Britton reserved a table together and instructed me to seat you both if they didn't arrive first."

Mitch watched Heather return to the front of the restaurant, letting her words sink in. "That's...*interesting*," he murmured, returning his gaze to his new table guest.

Nicole looked just as taken aback by the girl's announcement but slipped into the vacant seat next to Mitch to await their mothers. "Interesting, to say the least, considering I was expecting to have lunch with *my* mother." She hooked the thin leather strap of her purse over the back of her chair, then straightened in her seat to face him again. "She called this morning and insisted she had something important to talk to me about."

"Same with my mother," he replied wryly. "I can't imagine what the two of them are up to that they'd both conveniently forget to mention a foursome."

A naughty twinkle entered her gaze as she lowered her voice to a husky, teasing timbre for his ears only. "A twosome would be much more pleasurable, wouldn't you say?"

Heat rushed through him at her daring double entendre and, though he knew she was merely toying with him as she always enjoyed doing, he toyed right back. "Oh, most definitely. What do you say you and I slip out the back door and sate our hunger privately?"

"Ummm." The word rumbled provocatively in her throat, and she laced her fingers beneath her chin and considered his suggestion for a moment. "Sounds like a decadent proposition, but I don't think our mothers would appreciate walking in on the gossip we'd leave behind."

He laughed softly, humorously. "Your rebellious reputation precedes you, Nicole. You're not one to shy away from anything that causes speculation or gossip."

"Who, me?" Pressing the tips of her fingers to her chest, she tipped her head innocently and licked her glossy lips. The gesture made him wonder what her mouth tasted like deep inside. "Now what gives you that impression?"

Leaning back in his chair, he crossed his arms over his broad chest. "Oh, let's see," he said, mentally picking through the various escapades his mother had insisted on sharing with him throughout the years. He thought about the upset her breakup with Jonathan Gaines had caused, and since he really didn't know the exact circumstances revolving around that split, he found another episode to utilize instead. "What about the incident three years ago when you flatly refused your father's very generous offer to be a receptionist at his medical office—"

She interrupted him with expressive green eyes rolling heavenward and a very heartfelt, "Oh, *puleeze!* That 'generous offer' was my parents' attempt to mold me into a nice, traditional kind of girl, in a nice, traditional kind of occupation more suited for someone meeker and milder than myself." She feigned a very realistic shudder.

He managed to restrain the urge to laugh at her description which clearly contradicted her own outlook on life. "And not being a traditional kind of girl you instead went out and found yourself a business partner and shocked everyone by starting your own sports enthusiast business." Including her prominent councilman boyfriend at the time.

"All Seasons Outdoor Adventures, isn't it?" Mitch asked. From what he knew, she and her partner, Guy Jacobs, not only put together packages for clients interested in outdoor recreational activities, but the two of them were guides on various hiking and rock-climbing expeditions, white-water rafting trips, and other daredevil sporting events, as well.

"Yes, that's all true." Her chin lifted in a mutinous slant that matched the multifaceted spark brightening her eyes. "The business has been extremely profitable, not that my father has ever acknowledged my success."

And for some reason, her father's approval was obviously important to her, despite her attempt to pretend otherwise. The tinge of hurt in her voice was slight, but unmistakable, and was quickly concealed with an indifferent shrug of her smooth, tanned shoulder.

The woman apparently had a soft spot beneath that sassy, aggressive, sexy facade of hers. "Personally, you don't seem the receptionist type to me, either."

"Thank you." She beamed as if he'd given her a compliment of the highest degree, and lifted her water glass for a quick drink. "You know me better than I originally gave you credit for."

And damn if he didn't want to get to know her a whole lot better.

Unexpectedly, she leaned toward him and slipped her palm over the back of the hand resting on the table between them. His pulse leapt, and her smooth fingertips, chilled from the water glass she'd just touched, made his skin sizzle.

Her lush mouth curved into a smile filled with wicked intent. "So, shall we stroll out of this stuffy country club hand in hand like lovers and let our mothers come to their own conclusions when they hear the gossip about us?" She waggled her perfectly arched brows in a dare. "Could be tons of fun."

One thing was certain in Mitch's mind. If he took Nicole up on her brazen challenge and they ditched this luncheon, he doubted anything that happened outside this restaurant would be feigned. The vibrant fire in her eyes told him the attraction was real. And while she might pretend not to care about their mothers' speculation about them, he was willing to bet it was all an act. They both knew their parents would jump on the opportunity to encourage any interest between them, and he didn't think she wanted that, either.

He switched the positions of their hands, trapping hers beneath the heat and weight of his palm. His thumb rubbed the sensitive flesh between her thumb and forefinger, and she sucked in an audible breath.

He blinked lazily. "You know, I do believe you could tempt a saint to sin, and if it wasn't for both of our mothers heading this way at this very second, I'd call your bluff and see just how far you were willing to take this game of yours."

At the mention of their mothers' approach she subtly retrieved her hand so they weren't caught in such a compromising position. She sighed, a gusty breath of sound that held the barest hint of regret. "I guess we'll never find out just how far I was willing to take things, now will we?"

He stifled a grin and instead gave her a private wink designed to leave her a little unbalanced. "Not this time anyway."

NICOLE STARED at her lunch menu but was unable to concentrate on the array of entrées offered. While her mother and Joyce Lassiter chattered on about the fabulous sale at Bloomingdales they'd hit that morning, which had made them late for their lunch date, Nicole's mind spun with other, more distracting, matters—like the gorgeous, too-appealing man sitting beside her, their sexy banter, and her traitorous body's reaction to him and his arousing touch.

She drew a deep, stabilizing breath, which did little to alleviate the flutters in her belly. Mitch Lassiter always did have a way of shaking up her normally unwavering composure and generating feelings of restlessness that no man had ever evoked. He possessed the ability to turn her on with a look, a charming smile or just by speaking in that deep, rich voice of his. Not that she'd ever let *him* in on that intimate secret.

Her personal life was exactly where she wanted it to be, free of the kind of restraints and emotional entanglements she'd struggled with for the better part of her childhood and adult years. The only frustrating thing she had to deal with was the way her parents constantly compared her to her younger brother. Robert, who was working toward becoming a successful orthopedic specialist, had recently married a sweet, traditional kind of girl, and had a baby on the way. Being the oldest, and their only daughter, Nicole's parents had been pressuring her for years to settle down and get married. And if they'd had their choice, they would have picked her ex, Jonathan Gaines, to be her husband. An affluent councilman and socially connected, Jonathan was exactly the kind of man her parents would have adored for a son-in-law.

Unfortunately, Nicole's opinion on the matter hadn't mattered much. While her relationship with Jonathan had been more comfortable than exciting and she'd enjoyed his company and intellect, he, too, had harbored certain expectations of her...and she'd fallen short. Like everyone else in her family, he hadn't approved of her business venture, or her ideals, and he resented the time she'd devoted to All Seasons Outdoor Adventures. While there had been some relief attached to their breakup, it had also served as a painful reminder of how men found her independence and ambition too intimidating.

And then there had been her parents' astounded reaction over her split with Jonathan to contend with, especially her father's disappointment. He'd held her responsible for driving away such a prominent, solid prospect in lieu of pursuing what he referred to as a man's business. The entire incident had been yet another in a long string of disappointments for him.

But despite her past, and despite deeper, unsettled yearnings inside her now, she wasn't about to give up her hard-won independence for anyone. Not even Mitch. Occasional playful flirtations she could handle and walk away from, and so long as she didn't allow her encounters with Mitch to escalate beyond harmless, teasing fun, she'd be just fine.

With that lecture assuaging her mind, and feeling more in control of herself and her response to Mitch, she decided on a club sandwich and an iced tea, then placed her menu on the table to await their server. The four of them ordered their meals, and once the waiter moved on to a nearby table, Nicole picked up her linen napkin, spread it on her lap and regarded both of their mothers with extreme interest.

"So, what was so important that the four of us needed to have lunch together?" she asked.

The older women exchanged an excited look, then pinned their gazes on their respective children. Rhea was the first to speak. "We asked you two here today to ask for your help in aiding our charity work for Breast Cancer Awareness."

Mitch immediately sat up straight in his chair. His dark brown eyes, the color of rich chocolate, glimmered with concern as his gaze honed in on his mother. "Is everything okay, Mom?"

Nicole waited for Joyce's reply as well, knowing how crucial Mitch's question actually was. Seven years ago Mitch's mother had been diagnosed with breast cancer. While she'd recovered and had been in remission for years, there was always the chance of a reoccurrence. Nicole knew this all too well, since her mother's sister,

Andrea, had passed away from the disease. Her mother and Joyce had met at an emotional-support group and had been best friends ever since. In their spare time, which they both had a surplus of, they raised money and awareness for their favorite charity.

"I'm perfectly fine, Mitch." A bright smile reassured both of them of her exemplary health, and Mitch's relief was nearly palpable. "This request isn't for me specifically, but for the organization as a whole."

As the waiter delivered their drinks, Mitch sat back in his chair. The knit collared shirt he wore molded to his well-defined chest and toned biceps, and the bronze hue brought out flecks of gold in his dark irises. "You know I'll do anything I can to support your charities."

Joyce's face softened with maternal affection. For a woman in her late fifties and having endured many hardships, including the loss of her husband, she still looked beautiful and vibrant. "I knew I could count on you, honey," she said, patting her son's hand.

"You know I'll do the same, Mom." Nicole squeezed her wedge of lemon into her iced tea and stirred the liquid with her straw. "What do you need? A donation from All Seasons, or help in sponsoring a certain event?"

"You know I appreciate the offer," Rhea said as she brought her cup of hot tea to her lips for a dainty sip of her favorite herbal blend, "but this is something we'd like the *two* of you to do for us and the organization."

She and Mitch exchanged a perplexed look. Witnessing the bewilderment in the depths of his eyes, Nicole knew he had no idea what was going on, either. Their server arrived with their lunch order, and while he placed various dishes around the table and made certain everyone was satisfied with their meal, Nicole contemplated her mother's odd and very nebulous comment.

Mitch was the first to question it. "Mind sharing the details of this arrangement with *us?*"

"Of course." Joyce laughed lightly and dabbed at her mouth with her napkin. "Rhea and I came across an advertisement in the *Denver Post* publicizing a high-profile charity event and we immediately thought how perfect it would be if the two of you represented our organization."

Nicole took a bite of her club sandwich, feeling a setup of some sort coming on, but she was too intrigued by whatever elaborate plan their mothers had concocted to waylay their intentions until she'd heard everything. A quick glance at Mitch confirmed that he was equally curious to hear what this charity event was all about and what their involvement would entail.

"Go on," Mitch drawled.

Rhea stabbed a cherry tomato in her salad with her fork and continued where Joyce had left off. "There's this island resort off the Florida Keys called Wild Fantasy, and they're hosting an annual charity contest. The grand prize is one hundred thousand dollars that will be donated to the charities or organizations that the winners specify."

"And you want us to try to win that money?" Mitch guessed.

Joyce nodded enthusiastically, causing her silky, frosted hair to skim her smooth jawline. "Exactly. According to the rules in the ad, in order to participate in the contest the guests have to be single and willing to compete in a variety of events and competitions against one another to accumulate points and win one of three cash prizes."

"Sounds right up my alley," Nicole said, completely hooked on the idea. "And I definitely qualify on both accounts."

Mitch shot her a humorous glance. "Yup. You're single and you're definitely competitive."

She grinned sassily and wrinkled her nose at him. "And proud of both accomplishments, I might add." Indeed, growing up she'd honed those competitive skills all in an attempt to capture a smidgeon of the attention and approval her father had lavished on her brother. While her efforts hadn't gained her what she'd ultimately sought, they had made her a stronger, more independent person, as well as ensuring that she was always up for a challenge.

"Actually, you're both more than qualified, as well as our best chance at winning the money for the organization." Reaching into the bread basket for a roll, Joyce broke it open and slathered butter on the two pieces. "But this is more than a competition and charity event—it's also a vacation package. So either way you two should have a good time."

Mitch stopped his forkful of pasta halfway to his mouth as he stared at his mother. "Care to explain the *vacation* part of this?"

Joyce waved a hand between them, as if the details of that were insignificant. "Wild Fantasy first and foremost caters to guests' fantasies," she explained. "And while Fantasies, Inc. is sponsoring the event, the guests who participate will be treated to all the regular amenities the island and resort has to offer in their vacation packages. According to the brochures and information Rhea and I picked up from our travel agent, this place is a virtual paradise."

Nicole considered all the decadent possibilities inherent in a personal fantasy and knew she wouldn't miss out on the opportunity to indulge in a week of fun, sun and pure relaxation...and competitive games with Mitch.

"Sounds great to me," she said, making up her mind. "I haven't taken a vacation in over a year, so I'm sure I can work out something with Guy and get another guide to cover for me while I'm gone." She glanced at Mitch to gauge his response and to see what he'd decided, but he remained quiet and contemplative.

Rhea lifted her leather bag onto her lap and dug through the contents, withdrawing two separate folders. She handed one to Nicole and the other to Mitch, who reluctantly accepted the portfolio. "Since there are only a limited number of single guests allowed on the island to participate in the charity event, and we wanted to make sure you didn't miss out on this opportunity, we took the liberty of purchasing both of your airfares to Florida, along with your vacation package on Wild Fantasy. There's a questionnaire and application inside your folders requesting personal information that you'll each need to fill out before you get to the island."

Nicole thumbed through the colorful brochure, fascinated with everything the resort offered and promised their guests. Then she came to the questionnaire her mother had mentioned and the tempting phrase, *Where anything goes and anything is possible,* jumped out at her, as did the intimate question, *What is your fantasy?*

She bit her bottom lip in thought. If she was taking into consideration forbidden, erotic fantasies, the sinfully virile man sitting beside her fit the bill. Mitch Lassiter had been a part of her most private erotic desires for years, stealing into her dreams and fulfilling some of her most seductive fantasies in the darkest part of the night.

But beyond her favored sexual fantasy, there was something emotional she craved, a secret wish she'd harbored deep inside since she was a little girl. Unexpectedly, her chest tightened with insecurities she'd sworn she'd banished years ago when it had become apparent that she'd never live up to her father's expectations as her brother, Robert, always so effortlessly did. She'd given up trying to please her father and lived her life according to her own rules and expectations. Yet there was still that little girl within the strong, independent woman who wanted his approval instead of criticism. *Just once.*

Win or lose, she wanted to be appreciated for who she was and not for what she accomplished. That was *her* fantasy.

Her fantasy was simple, yet so intangible it was almost impossible to grant. But that wouldn't stop her from putting the request in writing—for her own personal, private reflection, not to be shared with anyone else.

Closing her folder, she met her mother's expectant gaze. "I'm game for a wild fantasy." Grinning, she turned toward the man beside her to gauge his response. "How about you, Mitchell?"

He shook his head regretfully. "Mom, I know how important this is to you, but I can't just up and leave the business for a spontaneous vacation."

"Sure you can," she refuted, placing her fork on her plate. "I already spoke to your brother, and he'd be happy to handle things for a week."

Mitch's dark brows creased into a deep vee at that bit of information.

"Quit frowning," his mother scolded gently. "I know you don't like me meddling in your business, but Drew agreed it was high time you took a vacation, since you haven't done so since your father passed away. And that was over eight years ago."

With a heavy sigh that echoed his hesitancy, he pushed his fingers through his thick, sable hair, mussing the strands in a way Nicole found incredibly sexy. Heck, everything about the man was inherently masculine and sensually exciting, enticing her in ways she had little defense against.

"I've been busy," he said, his tone a shade defensive.

"Exactly." Caring and kindness permeated Joyce's gentle voice. "Busy supporting me and putting both your brother and sister through college. What about doing something for yourself for a change? And in turn, you can do something great for our organization, too."

A startling warmth inundated Nicole, along with respect and admiration for Mitch and the responsibility he'd taken on since his father's death. He'd obviously abandoned his own wants and needs for his family's, yet he gave no indication that he begrudged the sacrifices he'd made to support them. It was difficult for Nicole to imagine her brother in the same position, making the same selfless choices, when he'd always thought of no one but himself.

She watched Mitch waver in his decision, looking way too serious when it was clear his mother desperately wanted him to relax and enjoy himself, away from work and obligations. Playing and having a good time was something Nicole knew how to do with flair. Having fun with Mitch, tempting and teasing him and driving him to distraction on a private island away from prying eyes, suddenly held a whole lot of appeal.

"Aw, come on, Mitchell," she cajoled in a sultry tone of voice that snared his attention and made him lift an inquiring brow her way. "Sounds like fun, don't you think?" Slipping off her sandal, she slid her bare foot beneath the hem of his pant leg and rubbed his muscled calf with her toes, teasing him. "Or maybe you're worried you'll come in second against me in competition."

The unmistakable dare hung between them. His gaze narrowed with a distinct but discreet message only she could decipher: *she was playing with fire.* In more ways than one. In her estimation there was nothing wrong with playing with his brand of sensual heat when she had no intention of getting close enough to the flame to get burned.

Yet scorch her he did when he caught the underside of her knee with his long, warm fingers before she could move her leg away. A sizzling spark ignited and flared upward. She intercepted a startled gasp before it had the chance to escape her throat, then had to swallow a groan of pleasure when he grazed the smooth flesh in the ultrasensitive curve behind her knee. With Mitch's help, she'd just discovered an erogenous zone she never knew existed.

And the wholly satisfied gleam in the depth of his golden-brown eyes told her he knew exactly what he was doing to her. Knew that with just a bit more pressure in the right place, she'd be putty in his hands.

She was beginning to realize what a formidable opponent Mitch was when provoked. She had no choice but to silently endure his blatant caresses and her body's feverish response to his touch or risk a scuffle under the table that would bring too much unwanted attention to their private battle of wills. So, with concentrated effort, she remained outwardly unruffled—a talent she'd perfected at a very early age—and waited for him to acknowledge her deliberate challenge.

He didn't disappoint her. "The very last thing I'm worried about is coming in second to *you*," he replied with a slow, lazy grin infused with a potent amount of confidence. With one last brush of his thumb against that arousing spot behind her knee—a soft stroke as tantalizing as a whispered promise of more to come—he released her quivering leg and shifted his gaze back to his mother.

"I'll do it," he announced in a steadier voice than she would have been able to summon at the moment. "Count me in on the vacation *and* the contest."

Joyce clapped her hands together in pure delight. "That's wonderful! Isn't that wonderful, Rhea?"

"Most definitely," Rhea agreed with an exuberant nod of her head. "We've arranged your flights so that the two of you will arrive on the island separately. Now, you need to remember to play the game like the rest of the contestants. You start off as strangers before pairing up for the charity event and competitions—"

"What do we need to pair up for?" Nicole interrupted, wondering if she'd missed an important part of the conversation while she'd been perusing the brochure and thinking about her own personal fantasy.

Her mother looked at her as if the answer to her question was obvious, but explained anyway. "The two of you are going to be a team."

"A team?" she echoed in confusion.

"Yes. According to the rules, single couples pair up as a team, and each person in the team wins half the prize money for their chosen charity. Obviously, the two of you together will increase our chances of winning the entire one hundred thousand dollars."

Of course. Nicole blinked, unable to argue with her mother's logic, even as she realized her mistake in believing that she and Mitch would be competing *against* one another. According to their mothers' plan, she and Mitch would be partners—a couple—and would have to rely on one another and their combined skills to win.

"It's all or nothing, Nicole. What do you say?" Mitch's deep, rich voice penetrated her thoughts, an indisputable dare in *his* tone this time.

All or nothing. The thought of spending one entire week in the constant company of Mitch Lassiter threw her off balance and caused a slow simmer in the pit of her belly. But there was no way she'd renege on her promise to her mother.

She summoned a bit of sass and attitude, just enough to boost her own confidence and resurrect personal boundaries between her and Mitch. "I say I hope you can keep up with me and don't slow me down during the events."

His answering grin assured her that he'd have no problem at all keeping up with her pace. "That's the last thing you'll have to worry about."

He was right. She was more worried about their attraction, and spending a week alone with him.

2

"LET'S SEE..." The overly voluptuous redhead in tight pink spandex licked her lips as her gaze raked up and down the length of Mitch's body. "If I had to take a guess I'd say that you're the male exotic dancer."

Mitch winced inwardly, having been pegged as a "stripper" by three different women in the span of half an hour. "No, I'm an auto broker."

"What a waste of a great body." The woman with "Rita" written on her name tag shook her head, obviously disappointed that he didn't take his clothes off for a living.

She glanced down at the paper in her hand once more, consulting the list of hobbies and individual interests each person on Wild Fantasy had contributed in order to participate in that evening's "singles' mixer." The event was a getting-to-know-you icebreaker to get everyone better acquainted with participants of the opposite sex before selecting their weeklong partner at the end of the night. If it wasn't for the fact that Mitch was assured Nicole as a partner, he might have changed his mind about this whole fantasy and charity business. The singles scene had never been his thing, and he'd yet to meet a woman he had any desire to spend an evening with, let alone an entire week.

So far, his experience on Wild Fantasy was proving not only to be interesting and surprisingly relaxing, but amusing as well. Other than being sized-up as a potential partner and possible plaything for the week, he was enjoying the luxuries offered by the resort and the fun, laid-back atmosphere of the island. He hadn't known just how badly he'd needed a vacation until the moment he'd stepped off the commuter plane and the tranquility and hospitality of the island had enveloped him.

He'd arrived earlier that day on a separate flight from Nicole. He'd spent the afternoon unpacking then walking the grounds, taking in the lush beauty of the island and familiarizing himself with the fabulous amenities included in his vacation package, a vacation that was his own private fantasy. One that had been incredibly easy to put into writing once he'd agreed to this spontaneous getaway.

He was going to thoroughly enjoy this week away from business and the real world. Leaving responsibilities and obligations in the hands of his younger brother had been extremely difficult to do after eight years of holding tight to the reins of Executive Fleet Auto Sales, but Mitch was determined to embrace a whole lot of fun, pleasure and all the potential this incredibly sensual island had to offer. He'd become used to taking care of everything and everyone else, but now he was going to do something for himself for a change, without an ounce of guilt or worry to hamper the experience.

And his decision to enjoy himself included finally discovering if the strong chemistry between him and Nicole could be taken any further than the flirting they'd engaged in for much too long. He'd refrained from asking her out on a date a few years ago, but this vacation afforded him a chance to make up for that regret, as well as the opportunity to pursue Nicole at his own leisure and in his own way.

All or nothing. Mitch had meant what he'd said, in more ways than just giving one hundred percent to the charity events and competitions. For years he'd sensed a depth to Nicole buried beneath a cloak of complex, multifaceted emotions he'd only seen glimpses of so far. Now he wanted to peel away each fascinating layer, until he revealed precisely what had molded this incredible woman into who and what she was. Not that he expected her to make the discovery process easy on him. He had no doubt Nicole would try to thwart his attempts every step of the way.

Rita looked back up at him, hope and excitement mingling in her eyes. "You're in the auto business, right?" she asked, repeating the information he'd just given her. "Then you must be the one who owns a Ferrari!"

"Nope," he replied, watching as her interest in him gradually dwindled with each question he refuted. "I drive a Ford Excursion."

Frowning at his choice of vehicle—she apparently preferred fast sports cars—she perused the list of data again.

Two questions down, one more to go, Mitch thought wryly. After the third wrong guess the general rule was to recirculate within the group of guests, unless there was a mutual attraction the two people agreed they wanted to explore further. No worry of that happening with Rita, thank goodness.

Rita lifted her gaze from her notes and graced him with a sly smile. "I bet you like to wear leather beneath your clothes, don't you?"

The restricting and very uncomfortable image that popped into Mitch's mind made him grimace. "Sorry. I'm strictly a cotton brief kind of guy."

"Too bad." Sighing in defeat, she moved on to another male guest with long hair, a goatee and a pumped-up physique. The first words out of her mouth were, "I'll bet *you're* the male exotic dancer."

Chuckling at the woman's relentless quest to find the stripper in the group, Mitch continued to mingle in order to look as though he was searching for his perfect match for the week. The variety of women he met ranged from sweet and shy to the more direct and brash. They exchanged information on their lists to learn more about one another, and while he found a few of the women very nice and likeable, none of them so much as kindled anything more than friendly interest.

The only woman he wanted to be paired up with was Nicole, and so far she'd done an exemplary job of avoiding him since arriving on the island. But as it was getting late and couples were starting to sign up as partners for the charity event, Mitch decided it was time to stake his own claim on the woman he desired—a gorgeous, sexy, spirited woman that would be all *his* for a week.

Strolling around the large, outdoor courtyard that had been set up for the welcome reception, he perused the crowd for a certain evasive, blond beauty. Torches illuminated the area, casting flickering light over the elaborate buffet of food and the dance floor, which was already half full with couples who'd paired off and were enjoying the soft rock tunes the band was playing. An occasional balmy breeze sifted through the palms and lush foliage, bringing with it the fragrant scent of tropical flowers and something more illusive and seductive...like wild, forbidden fantasies.

The familiar sound of vibrant, teasing laughter stimulated a very basic male response in Mitch—the kind of heated anticipation directly linked to Nicole. Glancing to the left, he found the object of his search flirting with a group of eager men vying for her attention.

Considering how fresh and energetic she looked, even after having spent the better part of the day traveling from Denver to Florida, he could easily see why those men had flocked to her. She was wearing a white eyelet top that played peekaboo with her flawless, tanned flesh shimmering in the torchlight, and the rounded neckline displayed her full, rounded breasts in a way that was enticing, yet innocently provocative. Slim pink capri pants hugged her hips, thighs and calves, outlining a centerfold figure, and strappy, heeled sandals boosted her height a few inches, making her legs seem endlessly long.

One of the men leaned close to say something to her, and another burst of amused laughter rent the air. Then she slanted the other man a coy look, and the possessive spark that jolted through Mitch took him completely off guard. He'd never been the jealous type with women, but much to his surprise he was feeling a tad territorial where Nicole was concerned. The sensation was a novelty, but one he didn't find at all intrusive. In fact, he welcomed the potent mix of desire and need she inspired, knowing he had a week with her to sate every emotion, curiosity and craving she evoked.

Giving the list of feminine traits, hobbies and interests one last cursory glance, and picking out the tidbit that best reflected Nicole, he sauntered up to the gathering and interrupted her little soirée. The three men hoping to claim Nicole as *their* partner didn't look happy to have yet another rival in their midst.

He made a place for himself next to Nicole and his arm brushed hers, making his presence known. "Mind if I join your group?" he asked her specifically, knowing the company she was currently keeping would object if they could.

She gave him a slow once-over and bestowed one of those dazzling smiles of hers on him, but there was nothing in her expression that gave away the fact that they knew each other. "Not at all. The more the merrier." She held out her hand for him to shake. "I'm Nicole Britton."

He slipped his hand into hers, savoring the soft, supple feel of her flesh against his rougher fingertips. He inhaled deeply, and the ripe, luscious scent of apricots assailed him. Despite having enjoyed a small feast from the buffet earlier, his stomach growled hungrily, but his sudden appetite had nothing to do with food and everything to do with her. She smelled good enough to eat, every bare inch of her, and he couldn't help wondering if her skin tasted as sweet and tempting as the fragrance teasing his senses.

He wanted to find out. Seduction and surrender played tug-of-war between their clasped hands and their clashing gazes. Nothing new there as far as the two of them and their attraction went. A lazy smile edged the corner of his mouth, and she watched his lips with a combination of fascination and guardedness. Her reticence made him even more determined to take this opportunity away from the real world, free from familial expectations, to explore what was between them.

His blood pumped heavily in his veins, and if the subtle way she tried to finagle her hand back from his grasp was any indication, she was just as affected by their silent, sensual exchange. And that was enough for him. For now.

Finally, he released her hand and introduced himself,

shattering that breathless spell that had held them both momentarily immobile. "Mitch Lassiter," he returned, following her lead in keeping their association anonymous. "Has anyone figured out which bit of personal information is yours?"

"Not yet." She tossed her head back in an attempt to restore her composure, and ticked off the failed guesses so far on her fingers. "I've been pegged as a model, someone thought I loved to travel abroad, and another person believed that I've jumped out of a cake for someone's bachelor party."

She grinned at the three other men, seemingly enjoying the fact that she'd stumped all of them. "Can't say I've ever done any of those things, but the last suggestion certainly sounds like a whole lot of fun."

And being the unabashed woman she was, it wasn't hard for Mitch to visualize her as a bachelor's fantasy, dressed in something skimpy that would show off her sinuous body. The only problem was, Mitch wanted it to be *his* fantasy she fulfilled. "Care if I take a guess of my own?"

She turned toward him, initially surprised by his question. Then she shrugged and an impudent light in her eyes replaced her hesitation. "Go right ahead. Give it your best shot."

Clearly, she didn't think him capable of nailing her contribution to the list of personal information he held in his hand. While he had no idea if his guess was accurate, it suited her competitive, athletic nature the best. "You've tried out for the women's Olympic swim team."

Her mouth opened, then promptly closed. He'd stunned her into speechlessness, which was a first between them. While he would have loved to rib her over that, he kept to their pretense of being strangers in front of their audience. The last thing he wanted to do was get them disqualified before they'd even had a chance to compete together.

"Wow," she breathed, her tone awed. "You're *very* good."

"So I've been told," he drawled, winking at her.

She sent her admirers a quick grin. "It looks like this is the guy for me. If you'll excuse us, I'd like to get to know Mr. Lassiter better."

The other men conceded defeat and broke apart to find other potential partners. The band leader announced that they'd be taking a break and that Merrilee would be arriving in a few moments to greet everyone and go over a few last-minute rules for the upcoming competition. The man encouraged guests to take advantage of the dessert buffet and open bar, and when Nicole did just that, drifting toward the table laden with various sweets and confections, Mitch followed, noticing her rare bout of quietness.

Nicole cast him a surreptitious glance as she picked up a small plate then selected a puff pastry with cream filling, drizzled with chocolate icing. "How did you know?" she asked, her tone so soft he almost didn't hear her question.

He tipped his head, not sure what she was asking. "How did I know what?"

"That I tried out for the women's Olympic swim team." She concentrated on choosing another dessert, this time opting for a small brownie square layered with caramel. "Trying out for the U.S. team was something that happened before our mothers met and became friends. Unless my mother mentioned it to Joyce, and she mentioned it to you."

There was something in her voice he couldn't quite decipher, something between hesitancy and insecurity, and he found it interesting that she wouldn't meet his gaze. "No, my mother never said a word, which means I doubt she knows anything about you trying out for the team. It was an educated guess, based on what I know about you. You're into sports and very athletic, so it seemed like a logical assumption."

"Like I said, you're very good, and intuitive." She licked a smudge of caramel from her thumb, her tongue slowly removing the sticky sweetness in a way that ignited a smoldering heat in Mitch's belly.

He wanted to know more, wanted to discover as much as he could about this complex woman and what made her tick. Including her drive and ambitions. "But this slip of paper doesn't say whether or not you made the team."

She visibly tensed at his comment and took her time savoring a bite of the pastry. "I never expected anyone to guess that information about me." Her reply was flippant, and very ambiguous.

"It's your own fault for putting that interesting tidbit out there for speculation," he argued lightly as he snagged a small lemon cheesecake square from the dessert table. "I guessed correctly, fair and square, so I think you owe me an answer." He bit into the sweet-tart confection and waited patiently for her reply.

Her chin lifted stubbornly, defiantly, in a way that was, no doubt, meant to waylay him. "Why are you being so persistent about this?"

He popped the last of his dessert into his mouth and chewed, not at all daunted by her terse tone. "Now that you and I are pairing up as a couple, I want to get to know you better."

The look she shot him brimmed with skepticism. *"Why?"*

His gaze swept the area, taking in the other couples laughing and conversing with each other. "Isn't that the purpose of this singles' mixer?"

"Maybe for those who *honestly* want to get to know one another."

"And if I honestly do?" he asked, his voice low and sincere, snaring her attention. He stared into her wide, searching eyes, letting his intentions toward her, his honest interest, dangle between them for a few consuming seconds. "It's a simple question, Nicole. Yes or no would cover it just fine."

Her straight teeth tugged on her lower lip, scraping off a crumb of chocolate. "How about yes *and* no?"

He chuckled and shook his head, not at all surprised by her answer that wasn't an answer at all. "How about you're being deliberately evasive?"

With a sigh she glanced away, making a production of setting her empty plate at the end of the buffet table. The flickering flames of a nearby torch illuminated the delicate lines of her profile, accentuating her natural beauty and making her suddenly appear vulnerable, which was a novel concept with Nicole.

Contradicting that too-brief glimpse of vulnerability he'd witnessed, she boldly found his gaze again. "I did make the team," she revealed, sounding proud of that fact. "But a week after qualifying, I shattered my wrist in a car accident. The healing process was excruciating and physical therapy took months. By the time I was ready to return to the team I'd been replaced."

Ahh, a fleeting victory that had been double-edged and bittersweet, he realized. Her regret was palpable, and he ached to reach out and offer a bit of comfort for what she'd lost. He gave in to the urge. With infinite gentleness he brushed back a few strands of hair that wisped along her silken cheek. His knuckles caressed her warm, smooth skin, and her breath hitched on a startled gasp, as if she wasn't used to such tenderness, as if letting someone get that close emotionally went against that tough facade of hers.

He was beginning to see traces of a much softer side. Despite her reserve with him, despite her sassy mouth, she was in need of a whole lot of tenderness, and touching, and the kind of understanding and acceptance that came without expectations.

And he wanted to give it to her.

"I'm sorry," he murmured, letting his fingers drift along her jaw before falling away. "That must have been rough."

She visibly shook off the melancholy that had overcome her. "Definitely disappointing. For me, and especially my father who had high hopes of me winning a medal." The smile that found its way to her lips did nothing to chase away the lingering sadness glimmering in the depths of her smoky green eyes.

She'd had high hopes, too, he realized. And he couldn't help but wonder how much of that longing of hers had to do with capturing a medal for herself, or pleasing her father. Before he could pose the question to find out, their host and the owner of Fantasies, Inc. arrived at the singles' mixer. Stepping up to the microphone, Merrilee smiled engagingly and greeted her guests.

"Good evening, everyone." A gradual hush fell over the crowd as she spoke, and all eyes trained on her. While Merrilee appeared to be in her mid-fifties, she was still a very attractive woman, with rich brown hair softened by gray highlights and kind green eyes that seemed very worldly and wise.

"Welcome to Wild Fantasy, where anything goes and anything is possible," she said once she had everyone's attention. "We have a whole lot of adventurous games and events planned on the island, as well as fantasies to fulfill, so let that phrase be your guide for the week."

Mitch silently accepted and agreed with Ms. Weston's philosophy—especially where Nicole was concerned.

"Tomorrow, the competitions begin." Excitement laced Merrilee's refined voice. "Just to remind all of you of the rules and guidelines of this charity event, once you've chosen a partner by the end of tonight's festivities, you'll be paired up with that person for the duration of the week. If you or your team member at any time decides to part ways because of personal differences, or if either of you chooses to decline any of the competitions or events, you both forfeit your place in the contest."

The strict rule made perfect sense to Mitch and no doubt kept discord to a minimum. It also forced couples to work through problems and differences. In other words, they had to compromise, an ability that was essential to any good, solid relationship.

He glanced at Nicole as Merrilee reiterated a few other basic guidelines, saw his partner's intense expression, and knew on a gut level she wouldn't break or bend any of those rules. She'd compromise with him and find some kind of common ground rather than relinquish the contest and prize money. Her perseverance was a strong trait that would work to their advantage.

"In a few days, by process of elimination based on scores, the teams will be narrowed down to the top seven finalists," Merrilee continued. "From there, the final round of competition will begin. This event will be much more difficult in execution and will require contestants to use mental and physical strategies to ultimately win one of the top three monetary prizes."

She paused for a moment, her gaze scanning the faces in the crowd in front of her. "But regardless of where you place in this contest, I want everyone to have a good time this week. And now that the band is returning from their break, you can enjoy the rest of the evening, find a partner for the contest and dance the night away."

Nicole watched the other woman step down from the platform and mingle with her guests and took a few extra seconds to shore up her defenses against the man standing beside her—especially after the way she'd opened up and spilled one of her biggest personal disappointments to him. She'd never shared that story with anyone.

What in the world had come over her? She'd learned at a very early age to keep her feelings under wraps in order to keep her father's criticism from stinging and her own strength and determination intact. She'd managed the feat successfully through her teenage and adult years, and even through her disastrous breakup with Jonathan. Yet Mitch, with his caring, dark brown eyes and startling tenderness, had managed to stir a deep yearning that threatened all the barricades she'd erected around her emotions. She could feel them crumbling, making room for more of that rare understanding and acceptance he'd offered. And that wouldn't do at all. Because, ultimately, her surrender would cost her what she she'd worked so hard for and treasured the most: her independence.

"Are you ready to head over to the sign-up table?"

The rich, deep timbre of Mitch's voice penetrated her thoughts, reaching past the loud buzz of rejuvenated conversation swirling around them. She chanced looking at him and her stomach did a little somersault at how tall, gorgeous and overwhelmingly male he was. Desire unfurled within her, a languorous kind of heat that slowly seeped through her veins and made her weak in the knees.

She wasn't ready to make a weeklong commitment to Mitch right then, even if it was all for fun and games. She desperately needed a bit more time to regain control between them before she relinquished even a small piece of her freedom for the sake of the charity contest.

"Not quite yet," she replied, and tossed a frivolous smile his way. "If I'm going to be shackled to you for an entire week as my partner I want to make sure you're qualified and competent."

His dark brows winged upward in surprise. "And what, exactly, do you have in mind to find out if I meet your standards?"

She thought for a moment and came up with the ideal way to test his skills, a match she was certain to win, which would put her back in charge mentally, emotionally and physically. "A game of darts in the lounge ought to give me a good indication of just how capable you are."

She turned to leave the mixer and head down the pathway leading to the lounge near the hotel, but before she could take her second step Mitch caught her arm and stopped her. His hold slipped lower, and the fingers encircling her wrist branded her, spreading a fiery, alluring warmth across her skin. His bold gaze beckoned to feminine instincts and she shivered, wondering how one man could have such a potent affect on her senses.

Instead of letting her hand go as she expected, he clasped their palms together. Skin to skin, he threaded their fingers in an intimate fashion, keeping her close. "What about me testing *your* abilities?" he countered.

The arousing rumble of his voice made his question sound like a sexual taunt that included all kinds of forbidden, delicious possibilities. Or maybe her mind and body were just so deprived that she was imagining the underlying innuendo in his words. She tried to draw a steady breath and failed to calm the riot of nerves clamoring within her. The brazen, tantalizing stroke of his thumb against her rapid pulse and the tenacity blazing in his eyes didn't bode well for the outcome of her latest challenge.

"You're just going to have to trust me and my abilities." She shrugged nonchalantly, though she was feeling anything but indifferent to him. "Or we could let our dart game speak for itself."

Grinning, he dipped his head, and a lock of sable hair fell across his forehead. "That hardly seems fair, since I'm a lousy dart player." No machismo on his part, just endearing honesty, and damn if that didn't appeal to her. "How about we test our skills *together* out on the dance floor, instead?"

3

THE VERY LAST THING Nicole wanted to do was end up in Mitch's arms, surrounded by his virile heat, his intoxicating scent, and his blatant masculinity. He gave her little choice in the matter and no time to issue a protest that wouldn't draw the unwanted attention of other people. Still holding her hand securely in his, he tugged her toward the parquet dance floor. Just her unfortunate luck, at that moment the band ended the fast tune they'd been playing and eased into a slow, romantic song one of the guests had specifically requested.

A heartbeat later she found herself wrapped in Mitch's solid embrace with her own hands gripping his arms in startled surprise. Any desperate ideas she might have had about stepping back to keep a few inches between them were quickly banished when he slipped his arm tight around her waist and pulled her firmly against his hard, muscular body. Automatically, she tensed, but her rigid posture did nothing to dissuade him or ward off her own awareness of him.

Every inch of Mitch seemed to be touching some part of her. His shoulders were incredibly broad, and her breasts crushed enticingly against his wide chest, making her nipples peak and harden and ache at the heated contact. Her belly aligned with his, and somehow, someway, he'd effortlessly managed to slide his jean-clad thigh between hers in a way that was completely natural to the kind of slow dance they were engaged in.

The gradual pressure he exerted there was deliciously exquisite. To her dismay, an insistent throb pulsed low and deep. The uninhibited beat of the music dictated the sensual rhythm of their bodies, heightening her own longing for something more carnal and forbidden with Mitch. The assault on her senses was almost more than she could bear, and she struggled to keep a tight rein on her physical response.

His free hand slipped beneath the heavy warmth of her hair, and the tips of his fingers brushed the nape of her neck. "Relax, Nicole," he murmured next to her ear.

Suppressing a telltale shiver of pleasure, she squeezed her eyes shut. Inhaling a fortifying breath, she summoned a convincing reply before she opened her eyes again. She pulled back, meeting his teasing, sexy gaze with a capricious grin of her own. "I'm perfectly relaxed, Mitchell."

Clearly, he didn't believe her. Doubts shimmered in his eyes, right along with something more devious. Sweeping a hand down her back in a long, meandering caress, he splayed his large hand at the base of her spine, right at the curve of her bottom. Lightning spears of sensation spiked through her and she stiffened at his penetrating touch, contradicting her attempt to pretend indifference to him.

One corner of his mouth tipped up in a knowing, beguiling smile. "That's hardly the response of someone who's relaxed." He pressed closer to her, if that was even possible when she already felt like a part of him. His gaze grew more intimate, his voice softer, but she had no problem hearing him above the band's entertainment. "Do I make you nervous?"

"Of course not," she scoffed, the automatic fib a defense mechanism to protect her emotions from this man.

"Then prove it." Indulgence and insistence warmed his eyes. "There's no one here that we know to watch us, so quit fighting what's between us and let your body soften against mine. Move with me to the beat of the music, Nicole."

His request beckoned to her, the kind of dare she'd come to expect from him. The current song ended, giving her the perfect opportunity to bow out gracefully with some kind of clever quip. But when the band cued up the next tune with a seductive, bluesy tempo, she changed her mind. As hot and restless as he made her feel, she refused to give him the power of knowing just how much he affected her. In fact, she was fully prepared to turn the tables on him and be the one to walk away from this challenge unscathed. Just to prove she could.

Blocking out everything around them, she captured his gaze in the dim lighting. Relaxing, she let the driving, pulsing beat of the music dictate the movements of her body, the sway of her hips, the shimmy of her shoulders and breasts, and the deliberate glide of her thigh between his.

Lost in the moment and unnoticed by the other couples around them, inhibitions and reservations peeled away. Nicole softened and flowed into Mitch, just as he'd requested. Through lashes that had fallen half-mast, she watched the flame of desire and need burn bright in his gold-brown eyes, just as she'd intended.

A surge of triumph welled in her, making her bold and too assertive. "So, what do you think, Mitchell?" she asked huskily as she smoothed her hands down his chest, experiencing equal measures of satisfaction and pleasure as his muscles rippled at her touch. Tossing her head back, she arched into him in a very suggestive manner. "Is this relaxed enough for you?"

"Most definitely." His free hand slid from her side, down past her waist and settled on her hip, leaving a trail of heat in the wake of his petting. "We're very good together, don't you think? Both of us qualified and definitely competent."

Nicole swallowed hard, unable to find the words to issue a sassy retort. She was too mesmerized by the irresistible, sexual allure in his raspy voice, too stunned by the depth of her body's craving for him to think, let alone speak.

Gently, he rocked her hips against him, igniting another frenzy of restless yearning within her. "The way we move together in such unison, the perfect fit of our bodies, is exactly the way it should be. Can you feel it, too?"

She felt too much. Every touch and illicit caress expanded the heat between them. Every slow, purposeful brush of his body against hers scalded her senses until she was burning with the kind of need only making love could assuage. It had been a very long time since she'd wanted a man that much.

She closed her eyes at that lusty thought but couldn't shut out his murmured words, which painted such erotic and vivid pictures in her mind. She saw them flesh to flesh, clinging to each other in a dance between lovers. Witnessed the perfect fit of their inflamed bodies. Felt him filling the achy emptiness in her. Felt her own thighs clench his much too shamelessly. Tension coiled in her belly and right where the pressure he exerted was the greatest.

A tremor shook her, a warning that immediately jolted her out of her daze. *"Stop."* The uttered command slipped from her lips before she could intercept it, and Mitch went still and quiet, though loud voices and music still swirled around them.

She blinked her eyes open wide, scattering the provocative images behind her lids. She stared up at Mitch in balanced increments of shock and mortification— and annoyance for his part in arousing her with his sexual monologue. Her breathing escaped her in soft pants, and she was feverishly hot, her skin flushed and tight.

Unable to believe she'd nearly allowed him to seduce her in such a public place, she attempted to untangle herself from his embrace. He held her secure, pinned against his athletic, all-male form, seemingly not ready to let everyone see just how affected *he'd* been by their exchange. She could feel his burgeoning erection between them, and another unwanted thrill raced through her.

She glared at him for turning what should have been a simple dance, an uncomplicated dare, into something far more tempting. "You don't play fair," she said, conveniently dismissing the fact that she was just as much at fault for provoking him.

He had no qualms about reminding her. "Oh, and you do?" he asked wryly.

Her chin lifted mutinously as her heart rate finally calmed. "You started all this, not me. I would have been satisfied kicking your butt in a game of darts."

Fleeting humor etched his expression, and he gradually eased them back into dancing to the song the band was currently playing, this time, in a more platonic manner. "At least we finally proved one important thing."

Curious, she took his bait. "And what's that?"

"How compatible we are." His tone was husky and soft, his gaze serious. "And that you want me as much as I want you."

She rolled her eyes at that, grasping for levity and a believable fib. "We're hardly compatible." She found it more difficult to deny his second claim, so she didn't even try for fear of him disputing her in sexy, tantalizing ways she wouldn't be able to fight. "We're complete opposites, Mitchell, and if it wasn't for the sake of this charity contest, we wouldn't be together right now."

"*Mitch*," he said unexpectedly, his voice vibrating with a tinge of frustration. His gaze turned equally intense. "For once, call me Mitch."

The sudden change in him startled her, but also made her more determined not to give into his demand. "Mitchell suits you much better." She fingered the collar of his red knit shirt. "Responsible, respectable and much too strait-laced for me."

Her blithe comment was meant to point out their vast differences and establish much-needed distance between them, but only served to spark a fierce, steely determination in the depth of his eyes.

Without preamble, he grabbed her hand firmly in his and pulled her through the crowd still enjoying the reception. He nearly dragged her down the dark, secluded path toward the beach, his long-legged strides easily eating up the distance while she had to use quick double-steps to keep up with him in her heeled shoes. Her head was spinning when he finally stopped where the walkway ended at one of the small shacks used during the day for guests to borrow beach towels.

Abruptly, he turned around to face her. Silver moon-light cast shadows over his lean, handsome features and made his eyes glitter with purpose. He was unadulterated male magnetism, raw and untamed, and a trifle dangerous. But it wasn't him she feared; rather it was her own electrifying response to all that strong-willed aggression.

Excitement and apprehension mingled. She'd met her match. She shivered at the thought, aware that they were very much alone. She could hear the faint, far-away voices of the people at the mixer and the crash of the waves on the shore behind her—or was that the frantic pounding of her heart against her chest that was echoing in her ears?

He stepped toward her, and she took a hasty step back—and found herself pressed up against the locked door of the shack. He moved closer and, before she could side-step him, he flattened his hands on either side of her shoulders, trapping her between hard, rough wood and his unyielding length. He didn't touch her physically, not yet anyway. But she could feel the simmering heat of his body and see the predatory light in his stare. While everything within her urged her to duck beneath his arm and bolt, she stood her ground.

She'd never been afraid of confrontation or conflict—she'd experienced plenty of both through her childhood and her one-sided relationship with Jonathan. She refused to retreat now, no matter how much this man continually evoked varying degrees of emotions from her. At the moment, wicked desire was most prominent.

"What are you doing?" she demanded, and wished her voice sounded more convincing, instead of so breathless.

He bent his head and skimmed his mouth along her cheek to the delicate shell of her ear, a riveting touch all the more erotic for what it promised. "I'm about to prove I can be just as reckless and daring as you," he said, his voice a ragged kind of velvet as dark as the night around them.

Her pulse quickened as she watched his full, sensual lips descend toward hers to make good on his word. She prepared herself for a wild, outrageous kiss—the kind of frenzied joining that would reflect their tempestuous relationship so far. Her posture stiffened, ready to divert his domination with some kind of defiant response.

She couldn't have been more wrong in her assumption.

With lazy deliberation, he brushed his mouth along hers, throwing her off-kilter with his featherlight, velvety strokes designed to soften her demeanor. Warm, delicate kisses to coax an ultimate surrender. And despite knowing she ought to do something to stop his slow seduction, her lashes fluttered closed and she rewarded his sensuous efforts with a sultry moan that was pure pleasure, without a trace of any protest.

Mitch knew the moment that Nicole was his for the taking, and experienced a surge of supreme satisfaction. This woman, for all her impudence and stubbornness and sass, couldn't refute the undeniable craving between them. Her warm, fragrant breath fanned his lips, intoxicating him with the ambrosial scent of sweet apricots and chocolate, a rare delicacy he had every intention of sampling deeper. Very, very soon.

Threading his fingers through the thick, silky strands of her hair, he smoothed his thumbs beneath her jaw to keep her face tipped up and her mouth poised right below his. Holding her slumberous gaze, he closed the distance between their bodies, gradually easing his hard length against her ultrasoft curves until he'd imprinted her from breast to thighs with scorching heat and pulsing awareness.

This time, it was him that groaned, at the rightness of this woman in his embrace, and the primitive need that gripped and consumed him. Done tormenting them both, he settled his mouth over hers. His tongue flicked out to taste and tease and gather the exotic flavor that was uniquely hers, and her lips parted on a breathy sigh, giving him the invitation he sought.

Tipping her head just slightly, he slanted his mouth across hers. His tongue delved deep inside in a slow, thorough invasion that was as sensual as it was possessive. He kissed her languidly, and with consummate, insatiable patience, until she grew pliant and just as needy as he.

He swallowed the raw whimper that rumbled in her throat, but there was nothing he could do to stop the restless way she moved against him. Not that he *wanted* her to stop, but she was making him harder and more aroused than he could ever remember being. She raised her hands, sliding them between their bodies—not to push him away, but to press her palms to the flat planes of his belly, explore along his waist, and caress the slope of his back. Her open and honest touch kindled a fever in his blood, caused his heart to beat a heavy cadence, and spurred him to higher levels of desire.

Their kiss turned hungry, rapacious—deep and wet and every bit as sexual as the currents arcing between them. Loosening the fingers of one hand tangled in her hair, he glided his palm down the smooth column of her throat and swept his thumb over the rapid pulse at the base. She shuddered and parried her tongue with his, leaving him aching with anticipation and overwhelmed with need.

Wanting to experience more of her, as much as she'd allow, he continued his downward journey and cupped the lush softness of her breast in his hand. She groaned and arched and offered more. He felt her nipple tighten and bead against his palm, and guessed that she was wearing a very flimsy bra—one of those sheer, lacy numbers that was more for show than substance. The erotic images leaping to life in his mind, combined with the reality of the moment, nearly sent him over the edge.

He rubbed his finger over the straining tip, wishing she was naked to his gaze, so he could take her in his mouth, finesse the budding hardness with his teeth and tongue, and taste her as he'd thought about earlier. A low growl erupted from him and he almost lost it completely when she skimmed her hands over the curve of his buttocks, clenched her fingers in the tight muscles encased in denim, and rocked her hips against his. Sensations bordering on pleasure and pain ricocheted through him, demanding he make a choice between release or restraint, and quickly, or else his body would make the decision for him.

There was nothing remotely responsible, respectable or strait-laced about what they were doing, as she'd accused him of being. Which reminded him of his purpose in seeking seclusion and deliberately playing this seductive game. Indisputably, he'd proved that he could be just as reckless and daring as her, but there was one other concession still left unresolved between them, and he meant to revel in that victory, too.

His breathing was harsh and ragged when he finally,

reluctantly, stopped the madness and broke their kiss. Instead of withdrawing completely, he let his lips drift along her jaw and down the side of her throat. Seemingly lost in the haze of passion, her head fell back to give him better access as he scattered hot, damp kisses up to her ear.

"Call me Mitch," he murmured, his voice a husky command. Nuzzling the sensitive hollow where neck met shoulder, he laved her fragrant skin with his tongue and wasn't surprised to taste the delectable essence of sweet, ripe apricots. He lifted his head and stared deep into her eyes. "Say my name, Nicole."

Her tongue slid across her lower lip, pink and swollen from their ardent kisses. "*Mitch...*" she complied on a hushed moan.

It was as much of an acquiescence as he could expect from her, and he'd take it for now. "I knew you had it in you, sweetheart. And now that we've established that we're equally competent and qualified, and extremely compatible, there's only one thing left to do."

As if she just realized what her palms were fondling, she dropped her hands from his buttocks and planted them flat against the wall behind her. The silvered moonlight highlighted the becoming flush that swept along her cheekbones. "And what's that?"

He grinned at her uncharacteristic show of modesty, especially after how uninhibited she'd been with him only moments ago. "All that's left is for us to sign up as a team, and then the games begin." He winked at her.

Grabbing her hand, he led her back to the reception, taking their return slow and easy so she could regain her equilibrium and so his own libido had time to cool. A few people eyed them, noting their reappearance, but considering this fantasy island and the charity's purpose was to bring couples together, he figured their tryst was acceptable. And it served to clearly stake his claim on the woman beside him.

Nicole was unusually silent and obviously distracted as they filled out the paperwork that would bind them together for the week. When he suggested that they enjoy a few more dances or find other entertainment on the island for the next hour or so, she politely declined his invitation.

"I think I'm going to turn in for the night," she said abruptly and tossed a saucy glance his way. "I suggest you get some rest, too. You're gonna need it to hold your own in the competitions tomorrow."

He chuckled at her parting remark, immensely relieved to see that their newfound intimacy hadn't altered Nicole's impetuous attitude at all.

HIS STROKING, skillful hands were cool on her hot, bare flesh, arousing feminine nerve endings to a fevered awareness. She reached for him, desperate to sate the empty yearning deep within her. Whispering her name on a soft groan, he covered her body with his, his mouth eliciting a heady rush of sensation as his lips and tongue found and lavished slow, exquisite attention on all her most sensitive pleasure points. Her breasts swelled and ached with each decadent swirl of his tongue along the velvety crest of her nipple, and the muscles in her abdomen contracted when his warm lips skimmed lower, and lower still.

The erotic touch of his mouth against her inner thigh, the damp heat of his breath, caused her to tremble. The caress of his tongue sent her to the verge of paradise and kept her poised on the threshold of a stunning climax. She shifted restlessly to try to accommodate him, but he'd somehow trapped her legs against the heavy weight of his hard thighs, keeping her from experiencing the ultimate possession of him burying himself deep inside her and pushing her over the sharp precipice of release....

Nicole awoke with a start. She blinked her eyes open to find herself alone in the king-size bed in her cottage, cheery rays of morning sunshine filtering into her room through the double slider leading to the beach. Her breathing was aroused and labored, her entire body throbbing with unfulfilled desire—a hunger Mitch had instigated last night, and one that had obviously carried over into her sleep.

She groaned at the injustice of having woken up before she'd had the chance to enjoy the end result of her sensuous dream. While she knew it would be incredibly easy to take the edge off the tension thrumming through her, self-gratification just didn't appeal when she was coveting someone else's touch.

Mitch's touch.

Hoping the gentle pulses reverberating through her body ebbed soon and on their own, she attempted to roll to the side of the bed to get up and realized her legs really *were* confined. The cool cotton sheets were twisted around her waist and ankles, which explained the sensation her mind had conjured. The early dawn breeze drifting in through the window fluttered across her skin and the silk of her chemise, accounting for the fleeting kiss of an ardent lover.

All fanciful illusions—not Mitch, as she'd imagined in her dream.

With a sigh of disappointment she wasn't quite ready to fully analyze, she untangled the covers from her body and slipped off the bed. At the moment, the best cure for what ailed her was a cool shower, and something to appease her appetite. Then she'd decide what she was going to do about the sexual cravings Mitch evoked.

After ordering a continental breakfast to be delivered to her cottage, she headed toward the bathroom and spied the sheet of paper someone had slipped beneath her door—an itinerary of the day's competitions and events. The schedule included more amusing games that would enable couples to become better acquainted, as well as earn points for their placement in the day's contests.

There was a three-legged race in the sand, a game that Nicole had excelled in at friends' birthday parties as a youth. Then tug-of-war across a pool of mud, which she was confident she and Mitch could win with their combined strength and strategy. And lastly, "How many times can you dunk your partner in the dunking booth out of twenty-four tries?" Ah, no problem there, either. She had aim and throwing capabilities that had been the envy of her teammates on her collegiate softball team. She grinned, already anticipating the satisfaction she was going to gain in that last event with Mitch at *her* mercy for a change.

It appeared she and Mitch weren't scheduled for any of the competitions until after lunch, which left her free and on her own to enjoy a little time sunbathing after breakfast. Anxious to take advantage of the island's warmth and hospitality, she stripped off her nightgown and took a quick shower. Twenty minutes later, refreshed and dressed for the day in a deep purple bikini and a matching sarong wrap, she sat out on her patio in the morning sun, awed by the gorgeous view of the ocean and indulging in fresh fruit, a buttery croissant and rich coffee.

Popping a juicy wedge of cantaloupe into her mouth,

she chewed the succulent piece of fruit. Unbidden, her thoughts drifted to last night and that hot kiss she and Mitch had shared—as if she could think of anything else! Not for the first time she berated herself for showing any weakness at all to Mitch. He was a man who unerringly knew exactly how to rattle her personal barriers, and she didn't like feeling vulnerable, in any way whatsoever. She'd learned that in giving another person any kind of power over her emotions she became much too sensitive, too eager for approval and way too easily hurt.

She took a drink of the most delicious coffee she'd ever tasted, savoring the smooth richness on her tongue. Not only was Mitch gorgeous and sexy, but she also found him to be unique and caring. It was an extraordinary combination that fascinated her, and enticed her way too much since she'd never yet encountered a man who possessed *all* of those qualities. Jonathan certainly hadn't cared about her wants and needs, but focused solely on his own.

But there was one important element that drew her to Mitch the most, and that was the fact that, unlike most men, he wasn't intimidated by her brashness—a defense mechanism that had become second nature to her since her breakup with Jonathan. Mitch gave as good as she dealt, didn't back off because of her aggressive personality and didn't feel intimidated by her competitive spirit or her fierce independent streak. There was no doubt in her mind that Mitch relished their debates and her challenges. Now all she had to do was figure out what to do about the explosive chemistry between them, yet maintain emotional control of the situation so she didn't tumble headlong into another relationship that would demand more from her than she was willing or able to give.

Ignoring their attraction would be the prudent decision to avoid complications, but when had she ever been sensible or judicious when it came to more reckless issues? She slathered a croissant with strawberry jam, smirked, and answered her own question: *never*. So why was she hesitating now to go after what she wanted—an affair with Mitch that would finally get him out of her system and purge thoughts of him from her mind?

She sighed as she took a bite of the flaky pastry, admitting to a slight flaw in her impulsive, reckless personality. Okay, so she wasn't Ms. Sensible, but neither was she a woman who'd ever propositioned a man. Nor did she indulge in brief affairs. *Normally*. But the circumstances of this fantasy island retreat were different, and there was no denying that she and Mitch were incredible together. Compatible in a way that had melted her resolve to resist him. Last night he'd shown her exactly why this tropical island was called Wild Fantasy, and he'd more than lived up to Merrilee's mantra.

"If anything goes and anything is possible," she murmured to herself, putting in words a new fantasy that needed fulfilling, "then I want Mitch Lassiter for the week." And she wanted him on *her* terms, where she remained in control. The different, erotic ways she desired him made her feel breathless and aroused all over again.

A grin curved her lips as the decadent idea entered her mind, a personal, shameless fantasy that excited her and would hopefully appeal to Mitch, too—if she had the nerve to express her desires and if he agreed to her request. She wanted him to be her personal love slave for the week, which was just about as wild as a fantasy could get.

It was the perfect plan, she thought giddily. A practical way for the two of them to embark on a consensual affair that would appease this hunger between them, without strings or any threat to her independent nature, and without the interference and expectations of their families. Just here and now pleasure. With her in charge and Mitch at her whim, she'd remain in control of her emotions while enjoying his attentions. After a week's time, when they returned to Colorado, they'd go their separate ways—without any demands or an unwanted commitment for either of them to worry about.

Yes, the perfect fantasy. What man could resist the opportunity to play sensual games and be part of a woman's deepest, secret wishes? And her request was just the kind of proposal Mitch would expect from someone who liked to live life impulsively.

She shored up her confidence to verbalize her fantasy, and crossed her fingers that Merrilee would agree to allow her a second, more intimate fantasy. With a deep, fortifying breath, Nicole headed back into her cottage to call Ms. Weston and, she hoped, to issue Mitch a challenge he wouldn't be able to refuse.

4

SITTING AT THE outdoor bar near the pool area drinking a frothy concoction of tropical fruit juices, Mitch covertly watched the woman who'd issued him one hell of a tantalizing proposition. Reclining on a lounge chair by the pool with the warm sun glistening off the sheen of oil coating her bare skin, Nicole looked like a goddess. His pulse beat a bit faster as he considered that appropriate description and all the different ways he imagined worshiping her body.

In essence, her shameless proposal that he be her love slave for the week was giving him permission to do just that. *If* he accepted her very enticing offer, which he'd yet to do.

When Merrilee had called his room earlier that morning and asked if she could speak with him privately, Mitch couldn't have guessed what their conversation would entail. Without a doubt he'd been initially surprised by Nicole's daring request, especially after the abrupt way she'd left him at the reception last night. He knew he'd given her a whole lot to think about after the seductive kiss they'd shared, but he should have known better than to think Nicole would retreat from yet another challenge between them. True to her character, she was dealing with the issue head-on and turning the tables on him so that *she* was the one in control.

Mitch munched on a handful of peanuts from a bowl

on the bar as he contemplated the situation and Nicole's proposal. There was no question that he wanted her— last night's kiss was a welcome release of years of pent- up desire for her that had tapped into something deeper for him he'd yet to fully understand. And he was definitely intrigued by her provocative request—a request that would allow them to explore their attrac- tion in ways they'd both avoided for too long. But there were personal issues for both of them to consider in her proposition, and he wasn't about to agree to her fantasy without knowing her ground rules first.

He shifted his gaze back to Nicole just as she mo- tioned to the pool waiter and bestowed a dazzling smile upon him. The young man wrote her request on a pad of paper while laughing at something she'd said, then headed back toward the bar to place her order. The bar- tender whipped up another frothy, fruity drink and placed the tulip-shaped glass on the server's tray. Just as the other man picked up Nicole's order, Mitch slid off his stool and intercepted him before he could leave the area.

"Would you mind if I delivered that drink?" When the waiter gave him a skeptical look, Mitch reached into his swimming trunk's pocket and tossed a few bills onto the surface of the bar to compensate the other man. "Nicole and I are teammates for the charity event and I'd like to make a good impression, if you know what I mean."

Understanding his reasons, the waiter promptly handed over the tray to aid what he believed was a ro- mantic pursuit. Mitch's intentions certainly qualified as that, and delivering Nicole's drink would also show her his willingness to be at her beck and call—if that's the way this particular fantasy played out.

Weaving his way around the other people enjoying the outdoor amenities, he came to a stop beside her lounge chair. Her eyes were closed as she basked in the sun, and he took a quiet, undisturbed moment to appreciate her full breasts and the sleek, slender curves of her body in a two-piece, vibrant purple bikini. His blood simmered in his veins, and before his desire for this woman became apparent to nearby guests he moved closer and stepped to the left, deliberately blocking the sun from her face.

Her long lashes blinked open at the loss of light and warmth. The friendly smile on her lips for the waiter she'd expected wavered when she looked up and saw that it was Mitch instead.

"What are you doing here?" Her voice was as tentative as the appraisal in her deep green gaze.

While she obviously possessed the nerve to make her sexy request to Merrilee, she was a bit more modest in directly confronting him. Judging by the uncertainty he detected in her expression, he couldn't help but wonder if she was worried that he might reject her proposition. He found her reserve endearing—yet another bit of softness that belied her normal sass and bold, spirited demeanor.

"I'm at your service, ma'am," he said, alluding to her fantasy request, yet drawing out the suspense of whether or not he'd agreed to her proposal. Grinning, he executed a bow and lowered the tray to her level. "I believe this is the drink you ordered."

Her eyes widened in surprise. "It is. Thank you." Sitting up straighter, she accepted the drink and took a sip of the froth on top of the whipped juice. Curiosity and anticipation mingled in her gaze as she took a longer drink, but when he offered no other explanation for his presence, she asked, "Did you see our itinerary of events for the day?"

"Yep." Setting the empty tray on a nearby table, he grabbed an upright chair and pulled it next to hers. He sat down and checked his watch. "Another hour and we're up for the three-legged race." Which gave them plenty of time to discuss her proposition.

A teasing smile tipped the corner of her mouth. "How are your coordination skills?"

He laughed at her blatant question, glad to see that competitive edge of hers sharp as ever. "If you're concerned that I won't be able to keep up with you, there's absolutely nothing to worry about. You set the pace and I promise not to fall out of step or trip us up." He stretched his legs in front of him and crossed them at the ankles. "Of course, if you don't have faith in my ability to keep in sync with you, we can always try a practice run."

She shook her head as she swallowed a drink of her juice. "I trust you." Her voice had grown husky, as if she was remembering last night's heated kiss that had been instigated by a similar challenge.

"I'm glad, because there's no reason not to." He wondered if she realized just how important it was that she did place her trust in him—especially if they decided to embark upon the private fantasy she'd requested.

"You trusting me, and me trusting you is imperative if we want to make it through all the competitions ahead of us," he told her. "We can't afford any opposition at all."

"You're right." She nodded in agreement and met his gaze with an abundance of honesty. "I have to admit that I don't like depending on anyone for anything, especially winning any kind of competition, but you'll have my full cooperation this week."

He sensed in her comment a deeper meaning than the simple issue of her independent nature, a more complex reason why she didn't like relying on another person. While his curiosity was definitely piqued and he wanted to delve past the surface of that nebulous statement, he decided there'd be plenty of opportunity later to pursue the issue, *after* they established their new relationship for the week.

Nicole swirled the contents of her glass, and a few dewdrops of condensation dripped onto her belly. She sucked in a quick, startled breath at the cold contact against her heated flesh, and Mitch watched in fascination as the droplets of water rolled downward and pooled in her belly button. She touched the wetness to wipe it away, and her fingers slid against her slick skin, smearing the trail of beaded dampness rather than drying it.

Arousal thrummed through Mitch. Feeling a bit wicked, and wanting to show her just what an attentive slave he could be, he reached for the cocktail napkin on the table next to her lounge chair and pushed her hand away so he could dab at the moisture.

"Let me help you clean up that mess," he said before she could object. The napkin immediately absorbed the water, and he dipped his finger into her navel to collect any last bit of condensation. Her belly quivered in response, and a lazy glance upward revealed the pearled tips of her nipples pressing against the thin material of her bikini top.

"I...I think you got it all," she said breathlessly, brushing away his sensual touch. She inhaled a stabilizing breath. "I take it you spoke with Merrilee this morning?"

Crumpling the damp napkin and tossing it onto the table, he leaned back in his seat and grinned. "Now *you're* the one who's intuitive."

"It was an assumption." She shifted restlessly on her lounge chair, a wry smile on her lips. "Twice now you've catered to my needs, in ways that go beyond polite protocol. I take it you've agreed to my fantasy request?"

"Merrilee told me about your proposition, but I didn't give her an answer." Relaxing, he clasped his hands behind his head, absorbing the warmth of the noonday sun through his cotton tank shirt. "I told her I wanted to talk to you first, and she said anything we discussed or agreed upon from here on would be just between you and I."

She tipped her head, regarding him speculatively. "I appreciate your discretion, but what's there to discuss? I thought my request was pretty straightforward."

He flashed her a grin. "It was, in terms of what *you* want."

She eyed him cautiously. "Pleasure and passion is a given considering the fantasy. Is there something else you want in return?"

"Just a few answers, for now." While he had no objections accommodating her specific desires, which would undoubtedly satisfy his own cravings for her, he'd like to think this affair would end up being a mutual liaison of give and take. Gut instinct told him that anything that happened between him and Nicole would be far from meaningless, but he also knew he had to tread cautiously where she was concerned. Despite her brazen request and headstrong personality, he'd detected nuances of a deeper wariness when it came to involvement with him, and the last thing he wanted to do was scare her off before they had the chance to explore their attraction on a more intimate level.

He posed his first question. "So, tell me, what changed your mind about us?"

She laughed, the sound light and playful as she set her drink on the table. "The answer to that should be fairly obvious, especially after last night." When he made no reply, her attempt at humor gradually ebbed. Her expression turned serious as her teeth tugged on her bottom lip. "Mitch...I want you to know that I didn't come to this island with the intention of seducing you."

"I know that." For all her flirting and teasing, she'd never given him the impression that she was the kind of woman who issued these kinds of sexy propositions often, if at all. Her hesitancy now spoke for itself.

"And the last thing I want is the complication of a serious relationship between us, first, because our mothers are such good friends and, second, because I'm not ready to settle down. I'm happy with my life the way it is, despite what my parents might think or want for me." Her fingers absently traced along the smooth plastic armrest on her chair, but her gaze remained steady on his. "We both know I'd be a liar if I said I didn't want you, but the only way I can do this is if we both agree to certain conditions."

"And one of those conditions is that you want a no-strings-attached affair." While it sounded like a perfect solution for both of them considering the different lives they each had waiting for them back at home, a little voice in his head wondered if just one week would be enough to appease his desire for her. If he agreed to her terms, it would have to be.

"Yes. It's a safe and practical proposition, for both of us," she said, championing her cause.

Safe and practical for *her*, to protect herself from anything emotional or long-term, and to keep her in ultimate control of their relationship. That much he was beginning to understand about her.

"Not to mention how exciting the idea of an affair is," he added, knowing that was part of the appeal as well.

"That, too." Her cheeks flushed, from the heat of the sun or their intimate conversation, he wasn't sure. "The best part is that no one would ever know what happened here on the island except us. Anything goes. In fact, pleasure can be our ultimate goal, besides winning the charity contest, of course. And once the week is over, we can return to Denver and go about our own lives without worrying about our families, or any kind of entanglements or expectations."

Mitch glanced toward the pool where a group of guests were playing water volleyball, taking a moment to mull over her perfectly executed argument before agreeing to anything. Her argument was solid, yet he had to wonder if she'd really be able to walk away so easily after a week together. And for that matter, could he? The answer to that didn't seem as cut-and-dried as it should have been.

He admired her candidness and directness in admitting what she wanted from him, even at the risk of him saying no to her proposal. But then again, he'd come to expect nothing less from her than openness and honesty.

And turning her down wasn't an option for him.

The promise of incredible pleasure beckoned, and the

words *anything goes* echoed in his mind, spinning the most erotic visions of him and Nicole together, making love and satiating every kind of hunger imaginable. But more than fulfilling the physical aspect of her fantasy, he saw her request as a golden opportunity to chisel his way through those emotional walls she erected between them when things became too intense. To discover a deeper insight into the woman who'd tempted him for years. To finally succumb to the desire and attraction they'd both skirted because of their families and see where it all led.

Mitch absently rolled his shoulders. He'd agreed to this vacation knowing he desperately needed a change of pace, knowing too that he needed to let go of some of the obligations that had restricted his life for so long. He'd taken care of his mother when his father had died, then again when she'd been diagnosed with breast cancer. He'd raised his baby sister, and put both her and his brother Drew through college. They were both grown adults with lives of their own. Now it was time for Mitch to grasp something for himself for a change. And Nicole was offering him the opportunity to make good on his own wild fantasy to embrace fun, pleasure and everything this decadent island had to offer. And that included indulging in this uninhibited, private time with Nicole.

He turned his attention back to her, saw the anxious light in her eyes as she waited for his answer, and decided to toy with her just a bit longer. "So, you're proposing that I be your love slave for the rest of the week, and we have this affair to get out mutual attraction to each other out of our systems?"

An adorably impish smile canted the corners of her

mouth as she gave an affirmative nod. "I thought the love slave part would be kinda fun."

Deep laughter rumbled up from his chest. "Keeps you in charge, doesn't it?"

She shrugged, neither admitting or denying his claim. "I thought most men like aggressive women in the bedroom."

He rolled his eyes, guessing she'd read that bit of philosophy in a women's magazine. "If that's the case, I'm not in the majority. When I'm with a woman I expect equal measures of give and take, in the bedroom and out of it. Though I'm not opposed to throwing in a little role-playing to make things more fun and exciting."

She contemplated his terms and expectations, then asked very cautiously, "What are *you* proposing?"

"Equality." Leaning forward in his chair, he reached out and touched her thigh with two fingers and slowly drew a squiggly pattern on her slick skin down to the inside of her knee, stopping just shy of that sensitive spot he'd discovered at the country club nearly a month ago. Judging by her quick catch of breath and the darkening of her eyes, he suspected he wasn't far from starting a public scandal.

Deciding any further exploration would require privacy and seclusion, he withdrew his fingers, braced his forearms on his knees, and clasped his hands between his spread thighs. The visible relief that etched her features did nothing to ease the obvious sexual tension he'd brought to life with his brazen caress. Mitch couldn't deny that he thoroughly enjoyed arousing Nicole's senses, and he had to admit he liked her completely and totally aware of him, as she was right now.

"No restrictions for either one of us," he continued, verbalizing his conditions. "I'll be your love slave and do anything you ask if you'll agree to do the same for me. I think that's a fair request since I have a few fantasies of my own I'd like to fulfill."

He watched her waver in her final decision, witnessing just how difficult it was for her to cede even a smidgeon of control to him. But he wouldn't consent to this fantasy without securing her full cooperation in exchange for his, and she knew it, too. She looked less than thrilled that he'd added a few modifications to *her* rules, but he remained firm, knowing she wouldn't let any change in her personal plan get in the way of what she wanted.

Luckily, it was him she wanted.

"We have a deal," she agreed.

MITCH DIDN'T KNOW the meaning of playing fair, Nicole thought, and for that he was going to pay, and pay dearly.

Picking up the first of two dozen softballs she'd been given to dunk her partner, she watched Mitch saunter over to the dunking booth to take his position up on the raised platform above the water. Drawing on fierce concentration, she rubbed her thumb over the taut leather covering the ball, savoring the heavy weight in her hand and the sweet retribution to come in their final event for the day.

It wasn't enough that Mitch had encroached on her fantasy, insisting that she surrender to his desires just as willingly as he would succumb to hers, he'd then proceeded to arouse her in subtle, sensual ways during the competitions. Or maybe she was just so attuned to him that everything they did, and even the simplest of touches, took on a sexual connotation.

Their first game, the three-legged race, had brought

every one of her senses to full alert. A two-inch velcro strap secured the ankles of one leg each together, and in order to keep their balance they'd banded their arms around each other's waists, bringing the sides of their bodies flush. Mitch had splayed his fingers on her bare belly for an extra snug fit, which had been a sizzling distraction that she'd barely been able to put out of her mind. True to his word, Mitch matched her pace and their long-legged strides fell into perfect unison. While other couples tripped in the sand and lost their balance, she and Mitch had claimed first place for all three matches.

Then there was the tug-of-war event, she recalled with a victorious smile. The first two couples they'd competed against had been easy wins, and just a matter of a few fierce tugs to pull them into the pool of slimy mud. The man in the last team, however, was a muscular hulk, but his partner was petite and prissy, which Nicole took full advantage of. While the hulk was extraordinarily brawny, her and Mitch's combined strength rivaled his and their match was a long, drawn-out battle that dragged both teams, in turn, right up to the edge of the mud before each gained control again.

Back and forth they went for what seemed like hours to Nicole. The muscles across her shoulders and down her arms had burned like fire, but no way was she going to lose this last round and her dignity in that vat of gooey mud. With a signal from Mitch and one last ditch effort, they'd dug their heels into the ground and yanked hard. With a muttered oath, the guy on the other end of the rope lost his grip, sending his female partner sprawling into the mud and him stumbling in behind her with a loud splat. The abrupt release of tension sent her and Mitch tripping backward, arms and legs flailing for balance and her grappling for leverage.

She latched on to Mitch on their way down to the grass. He tried to cushion her fall and ended up sprawled on top of her. The air had whooshed from her lungs and it had taken her a few extra heartbeats to gain her bearings, and her breath.

When the haze in front of her eyes cleared and Mitch's face came into focus, the first thing she saw was a wonderful concern and gentleness etching his features. And something warm and tender and needy unfurled within her.

He pressed his palms to the side of her face, his gaze searching hers. "Are you okay, Nic?"

Everything around them—the cheering crowd, the shriek of the woman who was covered head to toe in slime—faded away in that moment. The warm, solid weight of Mitch's body cradled intimately against hers felt decadent and seductive, making more than just her primary muscles ache. "Just a little dazed," she said, her voice a husky rasp of sound. "But we won."

He laughed, and the entire length of her body felt the languorous vibration. "Yeah, we did." Then a wicked smile spread across his full, sensual lips. "And just for the record," he added in that sexy, velvety drawl of his, "I like the way you feel beneath me."

A tiny tremor coursed through her, and she'd melted inside, softened, moaned...until he abruptly rolled off her and stood up, leaving her restlessly inflamed and determined to somehow, someway, even the score and seduce him in return.

"Are you going to stand there all day, or do you plan on throwing that ball? It's getting hot sitting up here in the sun."

Mitch's taunting voice snared Nicole's attention, snapping her back to the present. During her idle day-dreaming he'd settled himself on the platform above a good six feet of water. He'd also stripped off his tank shirt and, for the first time, she was given an unobstructed view of his spectacular bare chest. Her mouth went completely dry as she stared. He was rock solid, athletically built and absolutely magnificent. Those well-defined muscles along his arms, torso and abdomen rippled at the slightest movement, keeping her eyes riveted on him instead of the target she needed to focus on hitting.

"Come on, sweetheart," he cajoled, kicking up a playful spray of water with his bare feet. "Give it your best shot."

Strengthening her resolve, and her weak, wobbly knees, she narrowed her gaze on the bright red circle to the right of the booth, cranked back her arm, and threw the ball...and watched in horror as it sailed right over the target by a good foot.

She gasped, unable to believe she'd missed such an easy mark. And it was all Mitch's fault for distracting and provoking her! The crowd of women standing around the booth issued sympathetic words since most of them hadn't been able to hit the target, either. But it was Mitch's deep, amused laughter at her expense that annoyed her the most.

"You can do better than that, sweetheart." The sun glinted off his dark, thick hair, accentuating the mischievous twinkle in his golden-brown eyes. "The object of the game is to *hit* the bull's-eye."

She made a face at him. "Very funny, wise guy." She palmed another softball, collecting her focus. "Get ready to cool off, Mitchell. You're going to be spending a lot of time in that tank."

"Yeah, yeah," he drawled in a teasing tone. "Put your aim where your mouth is, and show me what you've really got."

Clenching her jaw diligently, she threw a fast ball, this time striking the target with unerring accuracy. A loud buzzer rang, the platform fell away, and Mitch plunged into the depths of water with a resounding splash.

She let out a whoop and did a victory dance while he climbed the rope ladder and positioned himself back on the seat for another round. Her sense of satisfaction for that small bit of revenge was heady. From there, she fired off the softballs, nailing every throw and beating the previous top winner by seven dunks.

By the time he hefted himself out of the tank after twenty-three consecutive dousings, he was laughing jovially. *Laughing*, of all things!

She watched him head toward her as he slipped his tank shirt back on, bewildered at his lighthearted, carefree attitude, having expected a more agitated response. In Nicole's experience, from incidents in high school with boys on up to her relationship with Jonathan, she'd learned that men found her athletic skills intimidating. They didn't like to feel as though a woman was smarter, stronger or better equipped to beat them at anything.

Not so with Mitch. The man was obviously very secure in his masculinity and had no qualms about letting her take the lead. At least in their competitions. Their seduction was another matter altogether, and one she suspected would be a constant game of one-upmanship.

Dripping wet, he wrapped her in a spontaneous bear hug that took her completely by surprise. He left her no choice but to cling to his cool, damp shoulders as he whirled her around and made her dizzy with his spinning and being pressed up against his body.

"I knew you had it in you." Finally, he released her. His gorgeous eyes sparkled exuberantly, matching the huge smile on his face. "You're incredible, Nic. Do you realize that put us in the lead for the day?"

Her mind stalled on his enthusiastic words: *you're incredible*. A lump formed in her throat, creating havoc with her rapidly beating heart. As silly as it seemed, his approval and praise meant more to her than actually winning the event.

She shrugged, not wanting to take all the credit or let him know how deeply his respect had affected her. "It was teamwork."

He combed his fingers through his saturated hair and waggled his brows at her. "So it helped that I egged you on?"

Clearly, he'd enjoyed doing so. "It was definitely an incentive to see you plunge into that water...*repeatedly*."

He tipped his head in amusement and brushed his knuckles down her cheek in a soft, feathery caress. "Not only are you incredible, but you're priceless, too."

His kind and caring touch, coupled with the sincerity in his words had a potent affect on her, stirring deep, restless yearnings that had no place in their arrangement.

"I skipped lunch and I'm starved," she said, changing the subject to something far more mundane. "How about you?"

He shrugged. "Sure, I could eat something."

"There's the buffet in the dining room, the restaurant

or the barbeque down by the beach," she said. "What sounds good?"

He spread his arms wide, indicating his attire, which consisted of wet swimming trunks and a damp tank shirt. "Since I'm not dressed for indoor seating, let's do the barbeque."

Fifteen minutes later, plates ladened with ribs, potato salad, hickory beans and fresh fruit, and a glass of fresh-squeezed lemonade in hand, they sat down at a vacant table in the shade near a tropical atrium complete with exotic plants, birds and even a few caged reptiles.

She watched him dig into his meal with gusto, his high spirits and buoyant disposition still amazing her. "For a man who just endured twenty-three repetitive dunkings, you look way too cheerful. I think you enjoyed that last event *way* too much."

A dark brow quirked over one eye. "Are you disappointed?"

For all her grumbling about getting even with him, she realized that she wasn't disappointed at all. How could she be when he'd been such a great sport? She shook her head and smiled. "No. Actually, the whole afternoon has been a whole lot of fun." And he was the reason she'd enjoyed herself so much.

"You're probably used to recreational activities, considering your business, but I can't remember the last time I've had such a good time." He picked up a pork rib with his fingers, his expression turning thoughtful. "I can remember times in my childhood when life was mostly about having fun," he amended, "but then I went off to college, my father passed away, and I found myself in charge of the family business and taking on responsibilities that were a bit overwhelming for a twenty-one-year-old kid. For the past nine years my sole focus has been all about taking care of my mother, putting my brother and sister through high school and college, and making sure they had everything they needed."

He was the one who was incredible, she decided, pushing her fork through her potato salad. He'd given up so much, possibly even his own dreams, to support his family. "Sounds like you really needed this vacation."

He licked a smudge of barbeque sauce from his thumb and grinned wryly. "I'm beginning to realize what an understatement that is. I underestimated the value of leaving work behind for playing and indulging in pure relaxation."

For as many years as they'd known each other, she really didn't know much about his private life. She discovered she wanted to learn more, as much as he was willing to share. "I take it you don't get out much, huh?"

"Probably not as much as I should." He gulped down half of his lemonade and started in on his hickory beans. "I play racquetball with a buddy of mine a few times a week and I jog in the mornings before work, but that's about the extent of my extracurricular activities."

A light breeze blew, ruffling through Mitch's drying hair like caressing fingers. Nicole wanted it to be *her* fingers threading through those soft strands. "I'm sure you date occasionally." As soon as the comment left her mouth, she realized that she'd spoken her thoughts aloud.

He swiped his napkin across his mouth and met her gaze. "'Occasionally' is putting it generously. I can count on one hand the number of women I've dated in the past three years."

His reply certainly took her by surprise. Judging by the dozens of covetous glances cast Mitch's way, she knew women found him attractive. And she possessed intimate knowledge that he was charming, exciting, sexy and damn near irresistible.

"Why?" she asked, another question she couldn't stop from verbalizing.

His forkful of potato salad stopped midway to his mouth, and his brows creased in a confused frown. "Why what?"

This was her chance to say "never mind" and take a huge step back from the personal territory she'd just jumped into. "Why don't you date much?" So much for playing it safe.

"It's not as though I'm not interested in women," he clarified, his voice infused with humor.

"I have no doubt of that," she murmured, having been the center of his very sensual attentions the past two days. She leaned back in her seat, feeling the tendons across her shoulder and down her arm beginning to stiffen from throwing all those softballs. No doubt, she was going to pay with sore, aching muscles later. "But it can't be for a lack of women being interested in you, either."

He shrugged off her remark, completely unaware of his appeal. "Honestly, I never had the time to invest in a relationship to make it work. Not a long-term committed kind of relationship anyway, because I've been too wrapped up in family obligations and responsibilities since my father's death. And, quite honestly, I don't like to do things halfway, in business or in my personal life."

A sudden frisson of unease skittered down her spine. There was a certain intensity in his gaze that put her on guard and made her wonder how his comment pertained to them and their agreed affair. Was there a deeper meaning to his words, or was she reading too much into his comment? She didn't know for certain, but she was determined to keep things between them uncomplicated.

A waiter came up to their table, and Nicole welcomed the interruption to their serious conversation.

"Are the two of you finished with your plates?" he asked.

"Yes, we are," she answered with a smile, and stood, ready to move on to something different. She groaned as her shoulder constricted with a twinge of pain that rippled all the way down to her elbow.

Mitch was instantly by her side, gently probing along her back and shoulder. "Hey, you okay?"

She didn't want to get used to his concern, his tender touch, but damn if she didn't like it. Too much. "I guess my arm is more out of shape than I thought." She grinned impishly, hating to admit even that little bit of weakness.

"Today's competitions were pretty physical."

Especially when he'd landed on top of her. Yeah, that had been plenty physical. Still feeling the imprint of his heated length, her body flushed at the provocative memory.

She pushed that sexy thought from her head. "I overheard someone mention that they have a great masseur on the premises. I think I'll go back to my room, take a long, hot shower, and try an in-room massage to relax my sore muscles." She stretched her neck from side to side in an attempt to loosen the taut tendons. "Want to meet up later for a drink or something?"

He strummed his fingers down her spine, and the light dancing in his eyes reflected pure devilment. "The 'or something' part definitely works for me."

5

AFTER OVERSEEING the day's competitions, verifying team scores and discussing placement and scheduling for tomorrow's contests, Merrilee strolled along the pathway leading back to the main hotel on Wild Fantasy. She had some paperwork to finish up in her private office before the day was over. Overall, she was very pleased with the progress of the charity event, as well as the budding romance and intimacy already developing between a few of the couples.

Like Nicole Britton and Mitch Lassiter. Ahh, those two definitely had potential and chemistry, Merrilee thought, breathing in the sweet, drugging scent of jasmine planted along the sidewalk. The kind of electric, primal attraction that couldn't, and wouldn't, be denied.

A smile touched her mouth as she recalled Nicole's phone call that morning and her bold fantasy request. Every guest was allowed one initial fantasy, but Merrilee always made exceptions for those who discovered they needed a bit more help in fulfilling other desires, especially when it pertained to matters of the heart.

Nicole's request wasn't an uncommon one on the island, and while Merrilee agreed to be the initial contact for the young woman's sexy fantasy, she'd left the final decision up to Mitch. Any agreement they came to would be a private matter between the two of them.

Over the years Merrilee had learned to read people and she trusted her instincts. Her business depended on her ability to delve past surface personalities that hid deeper vulnerabilities, and rarely did her intuition lead her astray. Despite the confidence and assertiveness infusing Nicole's voice during their short discussion, Merrilee had sensed an underlying hint of insecurity in her request, though at the time she hadn't quite been able to put her finger on what, exactly, it was that gave her that impression.

Her suspicions were confirmed, however, when she'd retrieved Nicole's application and read the personal, private fantasy she'd divulged before arriving on the island: *Win or lose, she wanted to be appreciated for who she was and not for what she accomplished.*

Nicole's fantasy was a very expressive one that no doubt had significant emotional scars attached. She sought unconditional approval and acceptance, even while she pretended that she was secure in herself and in control of everything around her—including her desire for Mitch. Indulging in a temporary, fun affair would satisfy her attraction to her partner, yet would maintain certain barriers that would keep him from getting too close. The way Merrilee analyzed the situation, Nicole was protecting herself from further hurt, and possibly feared that she wouldn't be appreciated for the soft, sensitive woman she was beneath that resistant facade of hers.

Wanting to make sure that the two of them were a good match and would complement each other's personal fantasy, Merrilee had also pulled Mitch's application and reviewed his request. He wanted to relax, have fun and enjoy a worry-free vacation after years of devoting his life to his family and business. An ordinary, straightforward, and uncomplicated venture.

But Merrilee had learned that most fantasies weren't that simple. She was willing to bet one of her island resorts that Mitch was hankering for a change, and possibly beginning to realize that something crucial was missing from his life—thus the permission he'd given himself to enjoy and let loose, to seize opportunities he might not normally grasp back home. Luckily for Mitch, there was a whole lot of self-discovery awaiting him, and Nicole was quite possibly a very important element in *his* fantasy, if he allowed himself to grasp that particular opportunity.

Merrilee had watched the couple interact today and knew they could learn from each other, as well as fulfill each other's fantasies. From what Merrilee had witnessed and surmised for herself, Nicole was outwardly strong-willed and impetuous, but Mitch's level, grounded personality balanced and complemented her. Neither saw that potential and how compatible they were just yet, but it was there beneath the surface, just waiting for them to unveil the promise of something rare and wonderful. And, if all went well, during the course of the week they'd do just that.

Knowing she'd done all she could on her end to bring the couple together, and that the rest was up to them and fate, Merrilee walked through the main entrance into the Wild Fantasy hotel. As if her thoughts had conjured Nicole, she spotted the young woman heading out of the sundry shop, a chilled bottle of water in one hand, and a plastic sack of snacks and goodies in the other.

Merrilee waved and stopped to chat. "I believe congratulations are in order for a job well done today. So far, you and Mitch are in the lead."

Nicole beamed. "Today was fun, but I'm sure the upcoming competitions and events are going to get much tougher."

"They do, but it wouldn't be much of a competition if all the events were easy."

"Very true," Nicole agreed, laughing lightly, her green eyes sparkling. "I'm looking forward to them."

Merrilee smiled. "So, are you enjoying yourself and the island?"

"Immensely. This resort is incredible." She gestured with her right hand to the elaborate lobby decorated with bird-of-paradise, a cut-crystal chandelier overhead and imported rugs covering the tile in the sitting area. Wincing in pain, she lowered her arm. "I think I overexerted myself this afternoon. I just made an appointment with the masseur hoping he'll be able to work out the kinks along my neck and shoulder."

"Bruce is the best we've got. You won't be disappointed." Merrilee regarded Nicole speculatively and brought up a more personal matter. "If you don't mind me asking, how did everything go today with Mitch and your request?"

A becoming blush tinted her smooth, flawless skin, hinting at secrets she wasn't about to reveal. "We came to a mutual agreement."

"I'm glad to hear that." Merrilee wasn't prying for details of their discussion—she only wanted to be assured that both of them were content and happy with whatever pact they'd made.

But before Nicole embarked on this endeavor, Merrilee felt inclined to share a few parting words. "Enjoy the fantasy, Nicole, that's what this island resort is all about. But most important, be sure to keep an open mind and heart when it comes to reality."

Several quick seconds ticked by as Nicole absorbed her words of wisdom. "You seem to know a lot about what your guests need."

"It's my job." She shrugged and smiled gently. "And I was once young and impulsive, too, and learned that you will rarely be steered wrong if you follow your heart's desire." Unfortunately, Merrilee had lost the one thing she'd ever desired, that one special man, and she didn't want her guests walking away from something that might change the course of their lives for the better. In the end, it would be all about the choices they made.

"Ms. Weston," Danielle, her assistant, interrupted breathlessly, her arms encumbered with stacks of papers and folders, "I'm very sorry to interrupt, but I have the itinerary for tomorrow you requested. We need to go over the times and events before I run off copies and have them distributed."

"That's fine, Danielle. Nicole and I are finished." Merrilee gave Nicole's arm a quick, affectionate squeeze. "Enjoy your massage and your evening."

Nicole grinned engagingly. "Oh, I plan to."

Merrilee headed back to her office, and wasn't surprised to find yet another fresh bouquet of ruby-red roses gracing her desk. Whatever island she was on, be it Wild Fantasy, Seductive Fantasy, Secret Fantasy or Intimate Fantasy, her "admirer" always seemed to know, and sent roses and usually some other small treasure every few days. She didn't need to read the card attached, either. She knew by memory what the note would say: *Because they're your favorite.*

Pushing thoughts of her mystery man from her mind

for now, she spent the next half hour consulting the itinerary with Danielle, making a few minor changes to the program before giving her the okay to circulate the schedule to all the participating guests in the morning. Once they were done, Danielle scooped up her stack of paperwork and turned to leave, and a leather-bound book slipped from the top of the pile and fell to the floor. Merrilee bent down to pick it up for her assistant since her hands were full, and froze when she read the familiar title on the old volume—a title that had been engraved in the deepest recesses of her heart and soul for over thirty years.

Her chest tightened painfully as the past rose up to greet her, something it seemed to have been doing so often lately. The book she held in her hand was a rare collection of poetry and sonnets by William Shakespeare. While that in itself was stunning because this particular volume was out of print and a collector's item, what was more shocking was the last time she'd seen a copy had been the day Charlie Miller had boarded the bus prior to being sent off to the Vietnam war. She'd tearfully pressed her favorite and much loved book into his hands, insisting he take it with him as a reminder that she'd always be with him in spirit, no matter how many miles separated them.

Heaven and Earth separated them now, his death still as fresh and sharp as if she'd lost him yesterday, instead of decades ago. And even though she'd often missed her favorite book of sonnets and poems over the lonely years that had ensued, she'd never been able to bring herself to purchase another volume because there were just too many painful memories attached to the book.

Drawing a shuddering breath, she ran her fingers over the gold lettering on the cover, faded from age.

The book she'd given to Charlie had looked *exactly* like this one...worn and creased and loved by its owner. She'd inscribed the inside front page to her one true love, and a shiver raced down her spine as she wondered if she opened the book whether she'd find the very same dedication she'd written all those years ago....

"Ms. Weston, are you all right?"

The concern in Danielle's voice pulled Merrilee back to the present. "I'm fine," she assured her assistant, then smiled to back up her claim. "I had no idea you enjoyed William Shakespeare."

"Oh, the book isn't mine," Danielle replied, quickly correcting her assumption. "It belongs to C. J. Miller. He had lunch at the café here on the island today after dropping off a guest and he forgot the book at his table. The waitress gave it to me and asked if I'd give it back to him the next time he was on the island."

Merrilee's mind reeled. The book belonged to C.J. She found that bit of information disconcerting, and admitted to being intrigued that he enjoyed the same kind of poetry as she.

And, it no longer surprised her that she'd once again missed meeting up with her elusive employee. But this book, and his evasiveness, only made her more determined to finally confront him face-to-face.

"I'll return the book to him," she said, making a split-second decision. And just to be on the safe side and to ensure that they *would* meet, she'd issue him a specific invitation he couldn't refuse. "Would you please send Mr. Miller a memo requesting his presence at the final competition and closing reception for the charity events at the end of the week? As our newest employee and the pilot who brought the guests to the island it would be nice to have him participate and be a part of the fare-well party."

Danielle nodded and jotted a note on the list at the top of her pile. "I'll deliver the memo personally first thing in the morning."

Once Danielle was gone and Merrilee was alone, she summoned the courage and dared to open the book to check the inside page for the dedication she'd written to Charlie...and laughed with relief when it wasn't there.

She was being silly, she told herself. Between C. J. Miller avoiding her and a secret admirer sending her some of her most favorite treasured things, and now the appearance of this rare book, was it no wonder her mind was playing tricks on her and provoking memories of the only man she'd ever loved?

Charlie was gone, lost to her forever in this lifetime.

C. J. Miller was another matter altogether.

THERE WAS no way Mitch was going to let another man put his hands on Nicole—not even a professional masseur. No, that particular pleasure would be all his, and by the end of their session, hopefully Nicole's as well.

If he was going to be her love slave he planned to do it right from the beginning. Tonight she'd be the center of his attention, her relaxation and enjoyment being paramount. He had every intention of taking things slow and easy and making her feel pampered and desirable...and completely in control of the situation and anything that happened between them. She might have faith in his ability to be a compatible partner during their competitions, but by the end of the evening his goal was to gain her trust in a far more intimate fashion, which he hoped would knock down a few of those emotional walls she was so good at erecting between them.

Satisfied with the sensual strategy he had in mind, Mitch headed up the cobblestone walkway leading to Nicole's private cottage. In the distance the sun was dropping over the horizon as twilight settled in, painting the expanse of sky in vivid shades of orange and red, highlighted with deep purple—an awesome sight to behold. Gentle waves lapped on the shore of the pristine, sandy beach, and the air around him stirred with the heady fragrance of jasmine, electric currents of excitement and the aura of sultry, forbidden desires.

Fulfilling sultry, forbidden desires were definitely on tonight's agenda.

After parting ways with Nicole earlier he'd gone back to his own cottage, taken a shower, and changed into jeans and a clean shirt. Then he'd decided to pay a visit to Bruce, the island's masseur, to cancel Nicole's appointment and to ask for some advice on the finer points of giving a soothing massage.

Now, armed with a wealth of knowledge and a small duffel bag filled with a few essential items he'd purchased from the resort's boutique that catered to everything from the more modest to the wildest of fantasies, Mitch knocked on Nicole's door.

Seconds later she answered, dressed in a comfortable, baggy pair of sweatpants with a cotton camisole, and her thick, rich hair piled on top of her head and held in place with a large clawlike clip. A few strands escaped and wisped along her neck, still damp from a shower. Her face was scrubbed clean of any makeup, and she looked wholesome and more beautiful than any woman he'd ever known.

Seeing him standing at her door, her expression reflected an amusing combination of surprise and confusion. "I thought we weren't meeting up until later at the lounge, or did I misunderstand our earlier conversation?" she asked, her tone bewildered. "I have an appointment with the masseur and he should be here any minute."

"You didn't misunderstand, though I did leave things between us open when I said the 'or something' part works for me, which this definitely qualifies as." He allowed a slow, provocative grin to ease up the corners of his mouth, a prelude to more seductive things to come. "And you're looking at your masseur."

Her gaze flickered down the length of him and back up, her honey-blond brows winging upward. "You're kidding."

He shook his head. "I figured this should be *my* job if I'm going to be your love slave, don't you?" Never mind the other truth, that the thought of another man stroking her skin, kneading her flesh, finding that sensitive spot at the back of her knee that was his alone made him feel more possessive than he cared to admit.

Before she formulated a response, he reached out and caressed his fingers along her jaw, then glided them down the side of her neck, along her collarbone, and finally followed the thin strap of her top to the soft swells of her generous breasts, which rose and fell with each breath she took. She wasn't wearing a bra—that much was obvious by the way her nipples tightened and pushed so enticingly against the cotton of her camisole.

God, he loved the way she reacted to his touch, so openly and honestly. In their affair, at least, there would be no physical reserve or inhibitions, and that was a very good thing.

"Besides, would you rather have a stranger's hands on your body, or mine?" he murmured.

Beneath the fingers still resting on her chest, right

over her rapidly beating heart, he felt a shiver course through her. Her eyes darkened to a velvet shade of moss at the subtle challenge in his question. "I like the way your mind thinks."

He dropped his voice to a low, husky pitch and winked at her. "I promise you'll like the way my hands feel on you more."

A spark of excitement ignited in the smoky depths of her gaze. "That's a promise I'd be a fool to turn down." Grabbing a fistful of his shirt, she playfully tugged him into her cottage, establishing a light and flirtatious mood.

Which suited Mitch just fine. He wanted this evening to be fun and sexy, and satisfying for her, too. As she'd stated that afternoon, Mitch had little doubt that pleasure would be their ultimate goal during the course of their affair. As for tonight, well, how far they went depended on her. Undeniably, she was willing to engage in whatever provocative games he wanted to play, and eager for whatever he had planned, but he knew Nicole's penchant for retreating when things became too deep and intense.

But he was a patient man who knew the kind of rewards that came with doing certain things at an unhurried pace. A luxurious massage was one of those things. Yielding to Nicole's uncertainties was another. The two went hand in hand in establishing that trust he wanted to gain, so he was more than willing to let her set the pace, and a lighthearted mood.

She propped her hands on her slim hips, her mouth curving into a mischievous grin. "So, where do you want to do it?" she asked, her tone as sassy as ever.

The words "do it" held a slew of possibilities, and heat poured through him as his mind fabricated a few images of them entwined and tangled...and *doing it* in erotic and varied ways. He cleared his throat and topped her teasing request. "I thought the best and most comfortable place would be on the bed, so lead the way."

She did, and he followed her through a small sitting area with a couch and fireplace to an adjoining bedroom decorated in soft shades of green, gold and mauve. Setting his duffel on the large, king-size bed, he unzipped the bag and dug through the contents for a few items he'd purchased specifically for her.

He found what he sought—a short silk robe and matching panties, both in a pale, shimmery pink color and trimmed in French lace. While the wrap would afford her a modicum of modesty when she stepped out of the bathroom, he knew the panties, once revealed, would be a pure, delightful torment for him.

He handed the garments to her. "Here you go."

She glanced from the intimate, sexy apparel he'd given her, then back at him, curiosity etching her features. "What are these for?"

"For you to change into." He rested his hands on her bare shoulders, then glided his palms down her arms in a scintillating caress, his gaze locking with hers. "I want as little as possible between your skin and my hands without you being completely naked." Without her feeling completely vulnerable for what he had in store. The panties, at least, would lend a semblance of safety and security, unless she decided otherwise. "As for the robe, I thought you'd be more comfortable with it on when you came out of the bathroom. At least until you're ready to lie down on the bed."

She nodded her gratitude, obviously appreciating the thoughtful gesture. For all her boldness, it seemed her candid behavior didn't extend to exhibitionism, and Mitch found that demure chink in her armor vastly appealing.

While Nicole changed, Mitch set up the bedroom and turned off the lights, transforming the room into a seductive lair complete with soft, romantic music drifting from the radio on the nightstand and half a dozen flickering candles that permeated the air with the scent of vanilla. He left the slider open so they could hear the ocean and waves outside, and a gentle breeze billowed the sheer curtains, all of which added to the soothing, sensual atmosphere. He wanted her mind and body relaxed, and every one of her five senses brought to life.

A few moments later, Nicole exited the bathroom wearing the silky robe that covered her semi-naked body beneath, her eyes wide with delight as she took in the results of Mitch's preparations. "Wow, I feel as though I've been transported to another world."

"We *are* in another world," he said, catering to that illusion, the fantasy, which tonight was all about. "A place where it's just the two of us, where your wildest fantasies can come true." He swept her a low, formal bow. "And as your personal love slave, I'm here to serve you, in any way you wish."

He saw the flicker of anticipation in her eyes, witnessed the quickening of her breasts against the flowing material of her wrapper. "I like the sound of that."

He drew the bedspread down to expose the sheet. Blinking lazily, he crooked his finger at her. "Then c'mere and lie down on your stomach and we'll get started."

Unable to resist that particular temptation, she followed his gentle order and moved closer. When she reached the side of the bed and her back was to him, she untied the sash and slipped out of the robe before climbing up on the mattress. Stretching out on her belly, she rested her head on her arms.

Mitch's fingers tingled at the thought of all the tanned, bare skin on her back awaiting his touch, mesmerized by the arousing sight of her pert bottom in those pretty panties that fit her to perfection. Not surprisingly, his body and unruly hormones stirred, and he reined in his own awareness and desire so he could focus on heightening hers.

Doing his damnedest to put his mind in a professional, detached mode for now, he straddled her hips from behind to give him the best leverage and position for a massage, keeping the heaviest of his weight resting on her bottom. Grabbing the bottle of scented massage oil he'd put on the nightstand, he poured a generous amount in the palm of his hand and rubbed them together until the oil was warmed and both of his hands were slick and ready to work their magic on her aching muscles.

He started at her neck and kneaded his palms and fingers across her stiff shoulders, down the graceful slope of her back, and up her spine again in slow, sinuous strokes designed to soothe and relieve excess stress. His nostrils flared as the lotion emitted an intoxicating fragrance, enveloping him with the arousing scent of ripe, heated apricots.

There had been a dozen different fragrant oils to choose from at the boutique, all scented and flavored, the saleslady had informed him. He'd specifically chosen this massage oil because it reminded him of how delicious Nicole always smelled. Rubbing her down with the lubricant was his first priority, tasting would come later, with Nicole's permission.

Focusing on his task, he continued the firm pressure, the penetrating motions of his hands and fingers playing across her bare, satiny flesh, enjoying every bit of the process. Her body visibly relaxed beneath his, and her moan of appreciation told him she was enjoying it, too.

"This...feels...*wonderful*." She sighed contentedly.

The candlelight flickered, casting a golden, incandescent shimmer to her skin. "Good, because it's supposed to feel wonderful, and relaxing."

"Mmm, that, too," she said, her voice a purr of sound that vibrated beneath the tips of his fingers caressing her back.

Silence fell between them as Mitch touched and rubbed without demand or expectation, easing tendons and maintaining a continuous flow with his hands that enhanced the heat and friction between his palms and her supple curves.

Nicole was the first to speak and break the quiet spell. "You know, after our conversation this afternoon, I was thinking," she murmured drowsily. "Since you admitted that you're in need of fun, you ought to consider booking a trip with All Seasons Outdoor Adventures."

He considered her suggestion and knew he'd accept the offer on one condition. "Only if you'd be my guide."

"You're not afraid I'd drown you on some whitewater rafting trip?" Amusement and the barest hint of a challenge laced her husky tone.

Chuckling, he scooted a bit lower, so his jean-clad legs bracketed her thighs and his groin nestled much too intimately against her bottom. With effort, he ignored the pulsing sensation settling low and deep. "Despite how many times you sent me plunging into the dunking booth today, I'd trust you with my life on a rafting trip." Gently, but firmly, he pressed the pad of his thumbs along the base of her spine and gave thorough attention to the muscle bisecting her back, reveling in the telltale shiver of pleasure that shimmied through her.

"You're a brave man, and much more trusting than most guys. They take one look at me as their guide and fear that I'm some helpless female who doesn't know the first thing about rafting, or whatever other expedition they've booked."

The underlying note of frustration that crept into her voice was unmistakable, not that he could blame her for feeling perturbed. "And what do you do when they question your abilities?"

"Luckily, I have Guy's full support when we come up against that problem." Another low groan escaped her throat as he loosened a particularly taut bunch of muscles just below her shoulder blade. "If a client expresses doubts about my qualifications or competence, they have two choices—placing their confidence in me as a trained professional, or requesting a refund."

Curious, he asked, "What's the ratio on that?"

She grew quiet, and he suspected there were a few failures she was having a difficult time admitting to aloud. Finally, she opened up, rewarding him with a deeper insight. "In the three years since starting All Seasons, I've had three men cancel their vacation packages because I was the guide. And then there are the occasional few who've expressed doubts about my abilities, but come to respect my training and experience during the course of their trip."

Hearing the pride and determination in her voice, he grinned, gliding the tips of his fingers down her sides to the indentation of her slender waist. "I'm not the least bit surprised that you managed to sway the skeptics."

"Thank you," she said, accepting his compliment. "I've spent most of my life trying to prove that I'm a competent, intelligent female who doesn't need to be coddled, and it's frustrating when a client does exactly that."

That comment explained a lot of her ambition and drive, but not the reason behind it. And it brought to light that competitive edge of hers, as well. She had little to prove to him, but that was something she'd have to learn on her own over the time they spent together.

Pouring more oil into his palms, he worked his way lower, skimming along the side of her hips and tracing the edge of her panties with his thumbs, then continuing his ministrations on her firm thighs. Despite how toned her entire body was from all her outdoor activity, she was soft, pliant and intrinsically female everywhere it counted. His libido recognized that fact, and this time there was no holding back the heat that surged to his groin and made him hard with wanting her.

He clenched his jaw, trying like hell not to think about the fierce erection straining the confines of denim and what he *wasn't* going to do about that particular discomfort. Tonight was about Nicole and her pleasure, not his, and he searched for another topic of conversation that would distract the deep, hungry ache unfurling in the pit of his stomach.

"So, if I were to book a trip with All Seasons, what kind of excursion would you recommend for a rookie like me?"

"Hmm." Lifting her head, she propped her chin on her stacked hands as she mulled over his question. "How about bungee jumping or skydiving?"

He cringed, his belly doing a little somersault at the images that flashed in his mind, both of which included being airborne at excessive heights and fast speeds. Okay, so he wasn't much of an enthusiast when it came to extreme sports. "How about skiing, or fishing, or even sailing?"

"You have no sense of adventure, Mitchell."

Uh-oh. She was back to using his full name, and despite her teasing tone he knew what that meant...she thought him too responsible, serious and stuffy. And maybe he was, to an extent. While he acknowledged that he needed to learn to adjust his lifestyle to accommodate more fun and play time and needed to cut back on his sixty-hour work weeks, he wasn't sure he was ready to jump, literally, into daredevil stunts.

"I have plenty of sense of adventure when it comes to certain things." Like her, and their attraction. Yeah, that was something he was willing to pursue to the extreme. Brushing his fingers along the back of her knee, he lightly grazed that sensitive spot that aroused her so easily, heard her breath catch in anticipation...and moved on to massaging her calves. "I just have no desire to risk my life for some vicarious thrill."

"I thought you said you trusted me to be your guide."

Mitch frowned. Now she was testing him, silently asking if it came right down to it, would he have the faith so few men had shown her? His answer to that would be an unequivocal yes, he just didn't believe he had to prove it by accepting a wild and reckless challenge.

No matter what his reply, it would be double-edged. If he said yes, she'd want him to back up that bravado by agreeing to one of the adventures she'd mentioned.

If he hedged, she'd lump him into a category of men he had no wish to be a part of. Right now, it was a no-win situation for him.

So, instead of committing himself to an answer that might incriminate him, he tossed out his own personal bit of philosophy on the matter. "I don't believe trust is something a person has to prove, but rather earn."

And that's exactly what he was attempting to do tonight, establish an intimate bond that would transcend any doubts or uncertainties she might have about them, or him.

Finished rubbing down her backside, he moved off her and the bed and stood at the foot of the mattress. He decided to up the stakes between them, which would require a whole lot of faith on Nicole's part. "If I've earned *your* trust in the past half hour, I want you to turn over so I can continue your massage."

6

WHY WAS SHE hesitating? Mitch's request wasn't a matter of her trusting him so much as trusting *herself*, and gathering the courage to bare herself physically to him for the first time. Of course she wore panties, which was the same thing as swimsuit bottoms, but her breasts would be completely revealed to his gaze. While she wasn't a blushing virgin, the thought of Mitch seeing her naked for the first time made her feel more vulnerable and exposed than she cared to admit. Because what Mitch thought of her mattered, in ways that tapped into insecurities she'd spent too many years trying to overcome.

Despite her best efforts to bury those painful emotions beneath layers of carefully constructed confidence, it appeared those uncertainties were still there, too close to the surface, just waiting to stir up trouble for her heart and independent nature if she allowed herself to fall hard and deep for Mitch.

Which wouldn't, couldn't, happen.

She closed her eyes and pulled in a calming breath, easily pinpointing the source of her problem with Mitch—he made her *feel* entirely too much. More than desire, more than burning, restless hunger, he managed to awaken emotional needs with his caring and understanding. And succumbing to those longings wouldn't do at all.

Shaking off the unsettling notions threatening to pull her under, she told herself she was being too sensitive. She and Mitch had agreed to a sensual bargain while on Wild Fantasy, a sexy, provocative pact that her self doubts had no place barging into. She'd do well to remember that.

"What's it going to be, Nic?" he murmured from behind her. "Turning over or calling it a night?"

He was leaving the next move up to her, and backing down wasn't an option. She'd asked for this affair, this fantasy, and she wanted to experience whatever tonight and this week with Mitch had in store. And right now, she craved his warm, skillful hands on her body again, touching, stroking, and whatever else he might be inclined to do.

Leaving misgivings behind and grasping the promise of passion, she rolled over and let Mitch look his fill. And he did, a lingering, thorough perusal that traveled up her slender legs to the vee of her thighs, seared across her belly, and finally appraised her full, aching breasts. He caressed her with his hot, masculine gaze made hotter and brighter by the cast of golden candlelight in the room, and her nipples tightened and peaked in anticipation of a more intimate contact.

Reaching up, she released the clip securing her hair atop her head and shook the thick mass until the silky strands were spread out around her face and shoulders. Tossing the clip aside, she relaxed her arms at the sides of her head and simulated a deliberately seductive pose. He devoured every movement she made. The muscles across his chest rippled and flexed with restraint, but the impressive erection nudging the fly of his jeans told her the wanting was mutual.

Her lashes fell half-mast, and her mouth lifted in a

sultry smile. "Finish what you started, slave." She purred the order, playing a role that made her feel heady, incredibly sexy and very powerful in her femininity.

The smile he gave her in return was nothing short of wicked. "Yes, mistress," he replied obediently.

He poured more of that rich, potent-smelling oil onto his palms, and starting at her feet, he pressed his thumbs into her arch to ease the tendons there, then gradually worked his way up to her calves. She gasped and rode the crest of a tantalizing shiver when he stroked his fingers along that breathtaking spot at the back of her knee, which elicited a carnal response even higher, where a slow, insistent throb was making itself known.

Much to her disappointment, he didn't spend a lot of time on that pleasure point. He continued kneading and rubbing his way upward, grazing past her thighs and outlining the edge of her panties to her waist, until finally he moved up and over her. He settled his knees on either side of her so that he was sitting astride her hips and the hard length of him pressed against her belly.

With an intense, sexy look etching his features he brushed his fingers over her quivering stomach, coasted around the plump sides of her breasts and grazed just below her puckered nipples, which made them contract even more. He teased and tormented her, and she bit her lower lip when he moved on without appeasing that particular hunger, but couldn't hold back the frustrated moan that slipped from her throat.

Not the least bit swayed by her attempt to make her exasperation known, he rubbed her arms and even her hands and fingers, coating her flesh with the fragrant, arousing oil. With slow, languorous strokes, he pampered her skin everywhere but where she ached the most. Her limbs grew lethargic from his meticulous massage, her skin feverish with erotic warmth. A thrilling pressure spiraled deep in her belly and radiated outward, increasing with every sensual pass of his hands on her sensitized flesh.

Soon, the desperation and need coiling in her became too much for her to withstand. Unbridled heat infiltrated her blood, and she shifted restlessly beneath him. "Mitch...*please.*" Her voice was soft, husky, *pleading*, and she was beyond caring.

Mitch sat up, letting his fingers drift reverently from the rapid pulse beating in her throat, to the equally frenzied, vibrant rhythm of her heart. Just a few inches lower and he'd have her breast nestled in his hand, right where it belonged. But for as much as he ached to feel her soft, pliant flesh against his palm, he didn't take that liberty...yet. He'd give this incredible woman whatever she wanted—she only had to say the words to take this session to a more intimate, fulfilling level.

"Tell me what you want." His voice was deep and coaxing.

She pouted, her lush lower lip puffing out adorably. Clearly, she hadn't planned on verbalizing her desires. While he found her playfulness amusing, he knew this was where things between them could get intense, where she could withdraw rather than admit her needs aloud.

He treaded carefully, keeping the moment light and sexy. "I'm your love slave, not a mind reader." His thighs clenched her hips a little tighter, and he trailed the tips of his fingers down her belly to her navel, dipping his pinky into the downy soft crevice. "How do I know what you want unless you tell me?"

She wet her lips, staring up at him with an obstinate glint in her smoky green eyes. "I want you to touch me."

He ran his thumbs beneath the fullest part of her breasts, a teasing touch that made her shift impatiently beneath him. "I *am* touching you, sweetheart."

Her gaze narrowed. "You know what I mean."

"I'm afraid I don't." He swallowed back a chuckle, knowing she wouldn't appreciate him laughing at her stubborn display. But this was one concession he refused to budge on tonight, and he set out to make sure she understood his conditions. "There are a hundred different places I could touch you, in at least two dozen different ways, so you're going to have to be more specific about what you want. Tell me where and how to touch you. Or, you can show me what you like," he murmured, drawing lazy, circular patterns on her flat tummy that made her shiver. "I'm at your service, and I'll do anything you ask."

She swallowed hard, and whispered, "Touch my breasts."

His smile widened in approval. Reaching for the bottle of oil, he drizzled a thin path from the valley between her breasts and down her torso, then caught the rich liquid with his palms before it dripped off her body. Their gazes connected and held in the dim lighting as he smoothed the slick lubricant into her skin. She moaned in gratitude when he finally covered her breasts and rasped his thumbs across her erect nipples.

Then she surprised him by covering his hands with her own and guided him on a very sensual journey that acquainted him with exactly how she liked to be touched and caressed and stroked. Closing her eyes on a blissful sigh, she ushered his palms down her neck and arched throat, plied his fingers over the rosy tips of her breasts, and coasted their splayed hands over the supple skin of her stomach, all the way down to where he straddled her hips.

She was lithe and sleek and graceful, and curved in all the right places. His nostrils flared as the succulent scent of apricots and womanly desires assailed him, eliciting a primitive reaction deep in his belly. Her skin shimmered from the oil and candlelight, and his mouth watered for a taste of her.

When their joined hands met the barrier of his jean-clad thighs, preventing an even more provocative exploration of her body, her lashes fluttered open. Her teeth pulled on her lower lip as she looked up at him, her gaze warm and liquid with sensuality.

"I'm thinking you have way too many clothes on," she said, impulse and longing infusing her voice.

"And?" he drawled, inviting her to elaborate.

An enamored smile tipped the corners of her mouth. "I want your shirt off so I can touch you, too."

Impatiently, she tugged his shirt out of the waistband of his jeans. Since her prone position limited her reach, he took over from there, stripping the cotton T-shirt over his head and dropping it to the floor at the side of the bed.

Her soft hands were immediately on him, gliding eagerly up his taut torso. She outlined the width of his chest with inquisitive fingers, then followed the sprinkling of sable hair that bisected his abdomen and tapered to a thin line that disappeared beneath the snap securing his jeans. He groaned deep in his throat as his muscles contracted and his skin caught fire, and groaned again when her palm brazenly slid lower over stretched denim and cradled his thick arousal in her hand.

Instinctively, he rocked against her snug hold, and realized his mistake when the acute friction elicited a fierce, undeniable hunger that demanded to be appeased. His body shuddered and quaked, warning him that another stroke would be the end of his restraint.

With a low growl he grabbed her wrist and gently pulled her hand away. She looked up at him with a searching frown, and he was quick to reassure her. "As good as that feels," he managed to rasp between his strangled vocal chords, "I'm not quite ready for this evening to end, are you?"

She shook her head, her cheeks flushed with high color. "No, I still want more."

He waited, saying nothing, doing nothing, giving her the time to realize that she needed to be more precise with her request. He wanted no modesty, shyness or retreating tonight.

She slipped her fingers through his belt loops and tried to tug him toward her. When he didn't budge, she blew out a soft, exasperated breath of air. "Come down here and kiss me, please."

He chuckled at yet another sultry pout. Obliging her polite order, he stretched out alongside her and eased a thigh between hers. Delving the fingers of one hand through her unbound hair, he rested his other palm on her belly, splayed flat and idle. For now.

Lowering his head, he seduced her mouth with lazy, tender kisses, then nipped gently at her bottom lip, coaxing her to let him delve inside. With an unraveling sigh she opened for him, meeting the bold stroke of his tongue, then willingly following him into the depths of intense, drugging desire.

The pleasure was too much, and not nearly enough. Pulling his mouth from hers, he brushed his damp, parted lips along her jaw and the slender column of her throat, scraping his teeth along her silken flesh. Panting, she threaded her fingers through his hair, trying to tug him lower, all to no avail.

"Mitch," she moaned fretfully, having learned just how determined he could be. "I want..." She swallowed hard before expressing her newest demand. "...I want your mouth on my breasts."

And just that easily he was there, satisfying her need, drawing her into the heat of his mouth and laving the stiff crest with his tongue—and he discovered that the oil did, indeed, taste like ripened apricots. Which made him all the more hungry for her, all the more anxious to lick and suckle her elsewhere.

His lavish, unhurried attentions drew a cry from her throat, and she arched restlessly beneath him. Capturing the hand still resting on her belly, she guided his touch downward, into the lacy waistband of her panties, until his fingers found her soft, feminine cleft. She was dewy with need, hot and silky against the tips of his fingers, and as much as instinct urged him to ply that nub of flesh with a sweet, sensual rhythm, he refrained. Gaining her trust was far more important than giving in to his own impulses.

With one last leisurely lick across her distended nipple, he lifted his head and met her feverish gaze. He said nothing. Words were no longer necessary. She knew what he wanted.

Her hips moved impatiently against the hand between her parted, trembling thighs, but he didn't oblige the silent offering. *"Mitch."*

His name sounded more like a curse than a plea, but he wasn't about to change the rules now that they'd come so far. Her jaw flexed obstinately and her body was strung tight, but what she didn't realize was that she was the one in complete control. The power was all hers, and he was the one at *her* mercy.

"Say it, Nicole," he urged softly.

Her breath shallowed as an unspoken contest of wills ensued. His against hers. After long minutes passed, her desire for the release he could provide became greater than her need to win this particular battle.

"Make me come," she whispered.

Rewarding her assent, he slid a long finger into her, exploring hidden depths and secrets with hot, slick strokes made slipperier by the fragrant oil still clinging to his fingers. He swept his thumb over her delicate, swollen flesh and tantalizing sounds of hunger escaped her. Her hips moved without inhibition; his own body pulsed and grew achingly hard. Despite his own discomfort, he found incredible pleasure in watching her response and the myriad of emotions playing across her features as he pushed her closer to the razor-sharp edge of sensation.

Her building climax rippled through her, and she gripped his upper arms as she shuddered and let go. She was the most beautiful sight he'd ever seen, her skin flushed, her breasts trembling as she called his name in a breathless cry of exultation and greed. Only when he'd wrung every last nuance of pleasure from her quivering body did he remove his fingers, but he still held her close.

She looked up at him, dazed and awed. He understood, because he was feeling the same thing. Brushing a few loose strands of hair away from her face, he smiled. "Is there anything else you'd like, mistress?" The game wasn't over, unless she wanted it to be.

"Yes." This time there was no internal struggle, no hesitation. "I want you to make love to me."

"I believe I just did with my fingers." To prove his point, he touched his still damp fingers to her mouth, spreading the sticky sweet moisture from the depths of her body and the scented oil across her lush lower lip. "But there's always my mouth, my tongue, my body..."

"How about all of the above?" A brazen light sparked in her eyes as she nipped his fingers, then was quickly replaced by concern. "Tell me you brought condoms."

"I'm nothing if not a responsible, reliable slave," he teased, making sure she knew those stuffy traits of his did come in handy every now and then. "I bought a box at the boutique. They're in my duffel bag."

"Thank goodness." She breathed a sigh of relief, then gave him a tempting smile he felt sizzle all the way down to his toes. "Do me a favor. Keep one or two stashed in your pocket at all times. On a huge island like this, there's no telling when one will come in handy."

He chuckled and eased off her and the bed, though it was a huge turn-on knowing that they could make love anytime, anyplace. "Your wish is my command," he said, retrieving the prophylactics from his bag.

Then he stripped.

She lay there, sated, and admired him with her slumberous gaze, watching as he quickly shucked his jeans and underwear and donned protection so he wouldn't have to worry about it at a more crucial moment. She crooked her finger at him to come closer so she could touch and explore as he'd done to her, but he shook his head.

"That's one request I'm afraid I'm going to have to refuse. I'll never last with your hands on me." Standing at the end of the bed, he leaned over her, grasped the sides of her panties, and dragged them down her endlessly long legs, completely baring her to his gaze. "Not this first time."

Her fingers fluttered over her breasts. "Next time then," she promised huskily.

"Oh, most definitely next time." Grasping her foot, he lifted her leg to his mouth and pressed a hot kiss on the inside of her ankle. His lips worked their way upward, feasting on her apricot-scented skin and suckling the flesh at the back of her knee until she squirmed and begged for him to stop.

He did, only because he had more unchartered territory to discover, and when he reached the apex of her thighs he proceeded to make love to her with his mouth and tongue. Lapping slowly, intimately, then delving deeply, he consumed the exotic taste of her...and she turned wild for him in the process.

In no time flat he brought her to the verge of yet another spiraling orgasm. But this time he wanted to be a part of her when she came, wanted to feel the tight clenching of her body around his. Moving up and over her and settling himself between her spread thighs, he bracketed her face between his palms and took her mouth in a deep, probing kiss, sharing the flavor of female essence and apricot nectar.

She groaned and wrapped her legs high around his hips, locking him against her and urging him downward. Helpless to resist her method of persuasion, he filled her with a quick, heavy glide, and was instantly consumed by sleek, tight heat and a need that transcended mere sex.

Momentarily stunned by the intensity of their joining, he lifted his head and stared down at her. She looked just as startled, just as overwhelmed. And then, as if fearing he saw too much, she let her lashes drift shut.

Frustration rippled through him, as did a whole other slew of inexplicable emotions. No woman had ever made him want like this, need like this, *ache* like this. And while he'd never expected sassy, stubborn, independent Nicole to be that woman, he wasn't about to ignore or dismiss what he was feeling. Neither would he allow her to shut him out because it was safe for her.

He caressed the soft warmth of her cheeks with his thumbs and brushed his lips across hers. "Open your eyes and let me watch," he rasped. "Let me be a part of your pleasure."

It took her so long to respond that he'd nearly resigned himself to letting her have her way. But then her lashes fluttered open, revealing eyes glazed with soft amazement. "No one has ever cared so much about my pleasure."

Instinctively, he knew she was referring to much more than physical pleasure, and damn if that didn't make him feel fiercely protective of her. "I care, Nicole. This isn't about you and me separately, but us, *together*."

"I like the sound of that." She ran her hands down the slope of his back to his hips, her smile more fragile than he'd ever expect from her. "Make love to me, Mitch."

And he did. Pinning her more closely beneath him so

they were so much a part of each other, he fulfilled her
final request. He slid as deep as he could, until she
gasped with the force of it, then retreated and thrust
harder, faster, creating the most incredible, breathtaking friction. Beneath him, she writhed and arched and
moaned, welcoming his driving possession, then finally
let go, trusting him to be there for her once she touched
back down to earth.

She came apart on a soft, shuddering cry, her body
gripping him with tight, voluptuous contractions that
urged him to let go, too. He plunged into her in a series
of hard, swift strokes, suddenly desperate to satisfy this
insatiable need to completely claim this woman who'd
driven him crazy for so long. A deep, guttural groan
welled up in him and escaped his throat as a powerful
wave of completion surged through his body. The rush
was dizzying, the force devastating, wiping him out in
more ways than just physically.

And he knew, despite their bargain here on Wild
Fantasy, nothing would ever be the same between them
again.

"MR. MILLER, hold on, I have something for you."

At the sound of the young, determined voice, C.J.
stopped just as he was about to duck back into the sea-
plane. He was due in Miami to pick up a few guests and
deliver them to Secret Fantasy. He watched as Merrilee's assistant, Danielle, hustled down the dock toward
him, waving a piece of paper in her hand.

She stopped beside him, breathless, her face flushed
from running to catch him before he left Wild Fantasy.
She clutched her side and gave a little laugh. "Boy,
you're a hard one to pin down."

He shrugged, though he knew exactly what she was

alluding to. He'd spent the past few weeks perfecting being evasive—wanting to be sure that he was doing the right thing re-entering Merrilee's life after so many years apart. "I fly between four islands at any given time, and my flight schedule is constantly changing."

"Yes, I know," she acknowledged. "This charity contest and the events are demanding more of my time than I'd anticipated, so I'm just glad that I didn't have to spend the day trying to locate you."

He narrowed his eyes behind his aviator glasses, latching on to the sense of urgency in her tone. "Is there a problem?"

"I have a memo for you from Ms. Weston." She thrust the note in her hand toward him.

Tentatively, he accepted the memo, quickly read the contents, then glanced back at Danielle in surprise. "She wants me present at the final competition and closing reception for the charity event?"

She nodded and smiled impishly. "I know this might sound silly, but I think Ms. Weston is beginning to feel as though you're deliberately avoiding her. I really think you should make the time to be there, for the guests' sake as much as Merrilee's."

A grin tipped the corners of his mouth, and he adjusted the cap on his head. "Doesn't sound like I have much of a choice, now do I?"

"As Merrilee is so fond of reminding people, we all have choices." Danielle's voice was soft and wistful and filled with belief. "It's just a matter of making the right ones."

C.J. drew a deep breath and exhaled slowly, knowing what his choice would be. Knowing, too, the moment of truth had finally come for him and Merrilee. No more secret gifts as her admirer, no more keeping his distance, and no more hiding behind aviator sunglasses and a battered Air Force cap. Even the mustache he'd grown to alter his appearance would finally go for their final face-to-face meeting.

He'd come back to Merrilee the same way he'd left her that fateful day when he'd been sent off to the Vietnam war—as *Charlie* Miller, and with love in his heart and hope for a brighter future.

Memories as fresh as yesterday assailed him, of how young and in love the two of them had been, believing neither time nor distance could separate them. Death was another matter, and when his fighter plane had been shot down and he'd traded his dog tags with an officer who'd been killed in order to survive being a prisoner of war, Charlie knew he'd be reported to loved ones as being dead.

His decision had cost him Merrilee, who'd indeed believed he'd perished and had married one of her father's colleagues during the time Charlie had been in captivity. Instead of causing Merrilee more grief by reentering her life, he'd made the painful decision to let things remain as they were, to simply let her believe he'd been killed during the war.

Their lives had taken different paths—with him meeting and marrying Evelyn and having two daughters of his own. While C.J. loved his wife and they'd had a good marriage, he'd never forgotten his first true love. A year after Evelyn passed away, thoughts of finding Merrilee had teased his mind, and with a little searching through the Internet, he'd discovered that her husband had died as well, leaving her a very wealthy woman.

He'd always known that his Merrilee had a generous, giving heart, and it didn't surprise him in the least to

Janelle Denison 113

learn that she'd spent her multi-million dollar inheritance on four lush island resorts that specialized in granting other people their fondest wishes and desires. Wanting to be close to Merrilee, to see if there was any possibility in rekindling their former passion, he'd signed on as Fantasies, Inc.'s new pilot. He'd spent the past two weeks as her secret admirer, wooing and courting her and priming her for Charlie's return.

Now, it was time to make good on the promise.

A sense of finality settled over C.J., and he embraced *his* choice and the feelings he still harbored for Merrilee. This time, he was going to make things right between him and the woman who should have been his. This time, he wanted to fulfill Merrilee's deepest fantasies, and provide a happily ever after for them.

He smiled at Danielle. "Tell Ms. Weston I'll be there."

7

NICOLE COULDN'T avoid Mitch much longer. While she wasn't wearing a watch, the brilliant sun dipping below the horizon indicated nightfall was fast approaching. That's when all entrants were requested to gather for dinner and Merrilee would be announcing the top seven contestants who would advance to the final round of competitions for the charity event.

With a troubled sigh, Nicole pushed the hammock that was made for two, but presently was only occupied by one, into a last lazy swing, hoping for a bit of tranquility before she was forced to leave her private sanctuary and face Mitch again at that evening's reception. Hoping, too, that she'd be able to straighten out her emotions and her composure so she could better handle their supposedly uncomplicated affair.

A tiny, strangled laugh shook her at that notion. The love slave she'd asked for and the generous, caring man who'd visited her last night were becoming two *very* complicated issues in her mind, not to mention her heart. And if last night had seemed like a distant, provocative dream, this morning had dispelled that illusion when she'd woken with a gorgeous, sexy, tousled Mitch in her bed, no longer a part of her dreams, but a fantasy lover come to life.

And, oh, what a lover he'd been, she thought, unable to stop the tingle of awareness that spread from her breasts to her thighs and still sensitive places in between. The man had been totally attentive, shamelessly sexual and completely devoted to her wants and needs. They'd spent the night fulfilling erotic fantasies, this morning sharing a steamy, most satisfying shower... and that afternoon losing three of the five competitions they'd participated in.

After their events, in which she'd royally botched their first-place standing for who knew what position, she'd bailed on Mitch before he could suggest they spend the afternoon together and sought solitude and quiet. After showering and changing into a fresh cotton dress, she'd found a secluded place to relax down the beach from her cottage, but her mind was anything but idle.

Her stomach bottomed out at the awful reminder of how she'd been unable to concentrate on what should have been the simplest of feats, mainly because she'd been so distracted by Mitch—the scent of him, his touch and provocative memories of their night together. If she believed making love with him would take the edge off the sexual awareness and tension she'd experienced around him for the past few years, she'd been sorely mistaken. Last night had only heightened her senses, making her more conscious of him and the pleasure they'd shared. And made her realize just how completely he'd unarmed her emotionally with his mental and physical seduction.

She slung her arm over her eyes, berating herself for having such little self-control when it came to Mitch. She was weak, unable to resist him on any level. That notion struck fear in her heart, because the last thing she wanted to do was allow this affair to escalate beyond anything more than fun and fantasies.

Last night, he'd demanded nothing from her but expressing her desires out loud so he could fulfill them. On the surface it had been a very noble gesture, and she'd given of her own free will. But what she hadn't counted on was surrendering to his ministrations when she swore she'd stay in complete control of the situation. And the maddening thing was, he'd put the power and authority in her hands, and she'd let the reins loose. Her loss of control had been proven today when she'd let her attraction to him get in the way of her goals.

Unwanted, her mind replayed the afternoon's events. She'd managed to perform well in the first competition, which had been a fun, lively game of "Guess Your Partner's Attributes." The object was to identify different parts of their bodies—the chest, belly and thighs. Having spent the night and morning up close and personal with those magnificent traits, she'd accurately pointed him out in the line-up of men every time a new feature was revealed.

While they'd been given maximum points for that event, their standing slowly spiraled downhill from there. The second game had been "Pin The Fig Leaf On The Hunk," and while Nicole prided herself on accurate perception and sense of direction, she'd been way off the mark—nearly a foot, to be exact. Blindfolded, her mind had spun images of Mitch naked, waiting for her touch. Unable to focus and with her hand beginning to shake she'd lost any chance at a straight aim.

Losing such a simple contest had instigated frustration and even self-directed anger for letting fantasies of Mitch distract her. Sheer determination and her fierce competitive spirit had allowed her to claim victory in the potato sack race, then lose again when it came to the wild and crazy "Clothing Exchange," which should have been filled with fun and laughter, but had been pure disaster for her. Stripping down to her bra and panties in a private dressing area hadn't posed a problem. Neither had throwing those articles of clothing over the partition for Mitch to put on in exchange for his shirt, shorts, shoes and socks sailing over to her side of the dual changing rooms.

No, her moment of failure had come the second she'd slipped his warm T-shirt over her head and she'd breathed in the mingled fragrances of woodsy cologne, earthy sweat and vibrant male—elemental scents she associated directly with Mitch and hot, carnal sex. Her body had responded on a very primal level to his essence, turning liquid and aroused. Her insides had clenched in a deep throb of excitement, short-circuiting her mind. Those extra ten seconds spent reliving last night's numerous pleasures had cost them any chance of salvaging the damage she'd already done by losing one of the previous events.

Her biggest downfall had been the orange pass, which required couples, their hands secured behind their backs, to transfer a dozen oranges to an empty bucket ten feet away—using only their necks and chins to pass the fruit to each other. How in the world was she supposed to focus on the task when their chins kept grazing, his hot breath tickled her ear, and her breasts continually brushed against his chest? She'd lost her hold on three of those twelve oranges, dropping their score even lower. By the end of the day she'd been near tears, and so very disappointed in herself for not being able to separate her emotions from her goals.

Nicole drew a shuddering breath. The way she figured things, after today's bungled performance they'd be lucky if they advanced to the final round, and the mere thought of not making the cut formed a huge, crushing pressure in her chest. While she accepted full blame for their drop in the standings, she knew she'd find it much more difficult to admit her failings out loud to her mother and father, when she knew they expected her to bring home the top prize. Her private fantasy was to be appreciated for who she was and not what she accomplished, yet now she feared criticism would come instead of approval.

Pushing those insecurities from her mind, Nicole peered at the glorious sunset one more time and gave herself a silent pep talk. No more hiding, no more avoiding. Now that she'd taken her brief reprieve from Mitch, it was time to confront her problem head-on, as she always did. And the first order of business would be regaining the upper hand in their affair.

Leaving her private refuge behind, she headed back to the reception area to meet up with Mitch. She arrived fifteen minutes earlier than the specified time, and while there were other guests mingling and choosing a place to sit for dinner, she didn't see Mitch. Finding a round table set for ten with a few vacant seats left, Nicole returned the smile of a pretty woman with short brunette hair and friendly brown eyes.

"Are these seats taken?" Nicole asked, gesturing to the unoccupied chairs.

"No, they're free. Please, join us. I'm Penny," the woman said as Nicole slid into the chair next to her. Then Penny glanced a bit shyly at the sandy-blond man sitting beside her. "And this is my partner, Graham."

Nicole noted the blush on Penny's cheeks and saw that the couple was holding hands. Obviously, the two of them had hit it off. "I'm Nicole, and it's nice to meet both of you."

"Where's your partner?" Graham asked, his hazel eyes reflecting curiosity behind the lenses of his wire-rimmed glasses.

"He should be here any minute." She scanned the area once more, but didn't see Mitch in the crowd. "After this afternoon's events we both went back to our rooms to rest and decided to meet up at dinner."

Penny nodded in understanding. "Graham and I are having such a great time. The events so far have been fun, but I have to admit that I'm not the most coordinated person in the world. Some of the competitions have been extremely challenging for me." She ducked her head after admitting that truth.

"I don't think you're the only one who finds the events challenging," Nicole rushed to assure her. While being uncoordinated wasn't a problem for her personally, Nicole had discovered that mental distraction could trip her up just as effectively as having two left feet.

"See, that's what I told you, too," Graham admonished Penny gently, then met Nicole's gaze. "I think everyone is under such pressure to perform and win in order to make it to the final round that tension and stress alone will cause mistakes."

While Nicole agreed with Graham's statement, she unfortunately couldn't use that convenient excuse for herself. She was used to performing under pressure, from her training and swim meets as a young girl, to her daily feats with All Seasons. There was no margin for error when she was responsible for another person's welfare, and while she claimed a clean record with her clients despite having come up against some treacherous situations, it seemed *sexual* tension wasn't as easily controlled.

"Well, I just hope we make it to the final round so we have a chance at placing in the top three positions." Penny's quick, meaningful glance at her partner was tinged with worry. "I'd really hate to let my brother down."

"Your brother?" Nicole asked, wondering what Penny's sibling had to do with the charity event.

"Tim was born with a heart defect, and my parents always knew that there was the possibility that he'd have to have a heart transplant." Penny's voice caught on painful emotion, but she managed to keep her composure. "About a month and a half ago his doctor told him and my parents that if he didn't receive a healthy heart for transplant within the next six months he wouldn't make it."

Penny swallowed the tears tightening her voice and continued. "He's only eighteen years old with his whole life ahead of him, and I want to do what I can to help my parents with the surgery and medical costs, which will be a couple of hundred thousand dollars by the time everything is said and done. So, here I am at Wild Fantasy, trying to do my best to claim a monetary prize."

Nicole's own heart ached at what Penny's family had endured. "I'm so sorry to hear about your brother, and I hope everything goes well for him."

"Thank you." Penny cast an adoring smile her partner's way. "If we win anything, Graham has decided to donate the portion of his proceeds to Tim's trust."

There was definitely a connection between the two, an intimacy and warmth that Nicole both envied and feared for herself because of all the emotional issues attached to such a relationship. "That's wonderful."

Graham slipped his arm around Penny's shoulders

and gave her an affectionate hug. "Yeah, well, I think *Penny* is pretty wonderful."

The color in Penny's cheeks deepened and she turned her gaze to Nicole. "What about you? What charity are you here for?"

Nicole explained briefly about her chosen charity and her own family's loss when her aunt had passed away from breast cancer.

Penny reached out and squeezed Nicole's hand, her expression sincere and kind. "That's a great organization to help. Good luck in making the finals tonight."

Nicole smiled, genuinely liking the other woman. "Best of luck to you, too."

The three of them spent the next few minutes exchanging mundane chitchat as their table filled up with other couples. Mitch arrived just as their waiter began serving their first course, a chilled salad with bay shrimp. He only had time to give her a quick smile and an apology before introductions were made again.

As everyone ate their salad, lively, humorous conversation ensued at their table—about the day's events and the botched attempts of other teams during various competitions. The level of noise, laughter and verbal exchanges finally quieted down when their lobster dinner was served.

That's when Mitch directed his attention to her. He leaned her way, so close she could smell his aftershave and the faint hint of mint on his breath. "So, where have you been hiding yourself for the past few hours?"

She slanted him a sidelong glance, deciding it was safest to revert back to her teasing, sassy attitude. "Miss me?" she quipped.

"Yeah, I guess I did." He sliced off a portion of his lobster and dipped it in drawn butter before meeting her gaze again. "I tried calling your cottage a few times and you didn't answer. I have to admit I'm curious where you spent your afternoon."

Surprisingly, she didn't bristle like she normally would have—as she had many times when Jonathan had called to check up on her or questioned her whereabouts when she wasn't at home or work. The difference was, Mitch's comment was motivated by concern, she knew, rather than the need to dominate or suppress her self-sufficient nature. In some ways his tenderness was equally dangerous to her well-being because she was way too drawn to it.

She shrugged nonchalantly. "I went for a walk on the beach and I found one of those comfy hammocks and just relaxed for a while."

"I would have enjoyed sharing that with you."

His voice was low and intimate, bringing to mind all that they'd shared the previous night. Reminding her, too, why she desperately needed to regain control of her feelings and emotions when it came to Mitch. "I needed the time alone."

He nodded, accepting her explanation without question. "Fair enough."

She ate a bite of tender, buttered lobster, savoring the delectable taste while struggling against the part of her that was softening and falling for Mitch in ways that were not conducive to the bargain they'd made to keep things casual and uncomplicated. Unbidden, memories of last night assailed her of how easygoing he'd been during her massage, and how she'd completely lost her grip on any semblance of control and had surrendered to him in ways she'd never, ever anticipated. As part of her fantasy she'd agreed to give him her body, but she'd never expected to plunge into emotional waters during the process. If she wasn't careful and didn't keep her guard up at all times, she was going to find herself in over her head and drowning, despite what a good, strong swimmer she was.

"Don't get your independent feathers all ruffled," Mitch said, interrupting her thoughts. "But I've been worried about you, especially after today's events and how upset you were when we parted ways. Are you okay, Nic?"

"I will be, just as soon as we're assured a place in the finals." The words fell from her lips without a second thought, and she turned away from his penetrating stare, suddenly hating the superficial way her comment sounded, how *she* sounded.

"Ever heard of the phrase 'winning isn't everything'?"

His tone was soft, reaching past that competitive attitude of hers—an attitude that had become an integral part of her life at an early age as she'd competed for her father's acceptance and approval. Her whole life seemed to have revolved around coming in first place and hoping for praise rather than criticism.

Her chest tightened, and she took a long swallow of her drink to clear her throat before she replied. "I've heard of the phrase, but I've never lived by that particular motto."

"Maybe you should." While his tone was low, for her ears only, his golden brown eyes held a sheen of purpose that burned deep. "Winning *isn't* everything, Nicole. Sometimes losing can bring great things, too."

She stiffened, unable to stop the automatic rush of defiance that surged to the surface and swirled with more complex, confusing emotions she didn't fully understand. A part of her wanted to agree with his philoso-

phy, but she couldn't bring herself to let go of old habits
and expectations.

Very calmly, she said, "Winning this charity event is
very important to me."

"But it's not just the money, is it?"

While his question was asked casually, it was laced
with too much certainty—and too much accuracy.
"Maybe I do want to win the charity event for more
than just the money," she admitted, wishing she didn't
feel so damned vulnerable in that moment. "But I don't
expect you to understand my reasons, Mitch."

A gentle, knowing smile curved his too sensual
mouth. "Maybe I understand more than you realize."

A frisson of unease skittered down her spine and settled in her belly like a ball of lead. Good Lord, she'd surrendered her body to him last night, but had she given
him a glimpse into her soul as well? The possibility startled her and preyed on her mind for the next half hour,
through the rest of her dinner and dessert, until Merrilee finally stepped up to the podium to announce the finalists.

A hush descended over the crowd as she greeted
everyone, but there was no denying the excitement and
anticipation that charged the sultry evening air.

"I know you're all anxious to hear who the seven finalists are, but before I make that announcement I'd
like to congratulate all of you who've made it this far."
Merrilee's smile softened her features and her eyes
sparkled from the flickering torchlight. "We've had
some teams drop out of the competitions, and from here
on it does get tougher. The seven finalists will be sent
off on a wilderness survival event on the other side of
the island for two full days. To make it through forty-
eight hours of roughing it, you and your teammate will

have to work together and rely on each other's strengths."

There were a few groans in the crowd on the heels of that surprising announcement, mostly from women who no doubt had no desire to be without all the luxurious amenities of the resort.

"You'll be supplied with basic camping gear, and a map outlining your camping area," Merrilee continued. "If you're spotted outside of your area, you'll be disqualified. You'll also be given a two-way radio for emergencies. At any time you can be rescued or you can request to drop out of the wilderness survival event if you decide you don't want to complete the forty-eight hours. But if you use that two-way radio, for any reason at all, you will be deemed ineligible to complete the event."

"Do we have to worry about bears?" someone in the crowd asked, which was followed by titters of laughter.

"I can vouch for the fact that there are no bears on the island," Merrilee stated, a mischievous glint in her eyes. "But there are plenty of other critters who do enjoy picking on campers."

A sophisticated, elegantly coiffed woman at their table squirmed uncomfortably in her seat, clearly not happy with the prospect of spending two days sharing her living space with rodents and other wildlife. Nicole stifled a grin, finding the other woman's delicate sensibilities extremely amusing.

"Whoever survives the length of two days on this venture will then advance to one last round of competition, which will determine the top three monetary winners. I do suggest that you use this time together to get to know each other on a more personal level, since the final event is a question-and-answer session." Merrilee paused for a moment as her gaze scanned her dinner guests. "And, as a word of warning, I checked the weather report for the next two days and there is a storm heading in that should be here by early tomorrow afternoon."

More adverse elements to deal with, Nicole thought to herself. And those opposing conditions would really test everyone's skills, strength and patience, as she knew too well from her own involvement with inexperienced clients on hiking and camping expeditions.

"And now, here are the seven teams with the highest scores who will leave the resort tomorrow at noon to begin their wilderness survival event." Withdrawing a piece of paper from an envelope, Merrilee proceeded to read off the finalists.

Nicole listened to Merrilee name the seventh and sixth place teams, not even realizing she was holding her breath until the other woman announced her and Mitch's standing in fifth place. The air whooshed out of Nicole's lungs, heavy with relief. She knew that the only reason they'd made it to the final round was because their high scores yesterday had balanced out their lower scores today.

Regardless, she was grateful, and more determined than ever not to screw up this second chance. Camping and wilderness survival was her expertise, which would put her back in control—physically, mentally and emotionally—for the next two days.

And if anyone was going to do any surrendering, she decided it would be Mitch conceding to *her* whims this time.

Penny and Graham placed fourth and, once all the teams were named, Penny jumped up from her seat and embraced Nicole in a warm hug. The other woman was so excited that bright tears of happiness filled her eyes. Something shifted and softened within Nicole, making her question just how important winning this event really was to her when another person needed that money far more urgently than her mother's organization.

"I've never been camping in my life," Penny said with a burst of animated laughter. "But there is no way I'm using that two-way radio for anything!"

"I'm sure you'll do great," Nicole said, offering as much encouragement as she could. She didn't have the heart to tell Penny that camping and outdoor adventures were what she did for a living, and risk deflating the other woman's enthusiasm.

"You're not alone," Mitch interjected, a wry grin canting the corners of his mouth. "I'm a city boy through and through."

Nicole raised an inquiring brow his way. "You've never been camping?"

"Nope." He winked at her, a sexy, flirtatious gesture that caused a riot of deep flutters to hatch and take flight in her belly. "I guess we could consider this our first outdoor adventure together."

A sense of satisfaction flowed through her. With his inexperience, and having him relying on her skills, she'd most definitely gain the upper hand.

His fingers strummed along her back, and he leaned close to murmur seductively in her ear, "What do you say you and I go somewhere private to celebrate?"

A shiver rippled along her spine and her breasts automatically swelled and tightened as if he'd caressed them intimately. The alluring gleam in his eyes told her exactly how their celebration would end—with them in bed and him buried deep inside her. For as much as her body craved that connection and pleasure with him, right now she was still feeling too confused and vulnerable after last night, and a bit fearful that she wouldn't be able to maintain that control she so desperately needed between them.

"I think I'll pass," she said, the regret in her voice genuine. "We didn't get much sleep last night, and I really need to start the day off tomorrow with a full eight hours sleep."

He nodded, his features etched with understanding, as if he knew she needed more time alone. "Consider your wish granted."

When the festivities and excitement of the evening died down, Mitch escorted her back to her cottage, both of them silent on the walk. Once they stood on her doorstep, he brushed his lips across her temple—a chaste, tender kiss that made her heart catch with a strong, undeniable yearning to hold tight to this man and never let go.

Startled by that unexpected, overwhelming emotion, she stepped back before she did just that. "Good night, Mitch."

"G'night," he replied, his voice husky and just as sensual as the smile on his lips. "If I can't spend the night with you, be sure to dream of me."

And she did...all night long.

8

"WHAT DO YOU THINK?" Mitch asked, motioning to a wooded area with a small, grassy clearing. "Does this look like a good place to set up camp for the night?"

Nicole shook her head as she consulted the map they'd been given that morning before heading out at noon for their wilderness survival event. "I want to find something on higher ground so we won't get washed out by the rain. Let's head up this path a bit farther." Glancing at the compass in her other hand, she trudged on, following the trail eastward.

Readjusting the padded straps of his backpack on his shoulders, Mitch cast a skeptical eye at the lead-gray clouds overhead that had moved in very quickly over the past hour. Humidity and moisture hung in the air, mingling with the scents of warm, damp earth and leaves. "It doesn't look like we have much time before that storm hits."

She waved away his concern, even as a rumble of thunder echoed in the distance. "We've got plenty of time."

He exhaled roughly beneath his breath and conceded to her obstinate attitude. "Okay...you're the expert."

They continued on, with Mitch doing his best to keep up with Nicole's unrelenting pace. She navigated the moderate terrain with ease, and though Mitch considered himself in good shape physically, he could swear they were walking in circles. He'd begun to suspect that the reason for diligence had a lot to do with not wanting to stop and deal with them as a couple.

After organizing their backpacks at the resort this morning with the supplied basic essentials—from food, to appropriate clothing and hiking boots, to sleeping gear and a small two-person tent—they'd set out for their forty-eight hour challenge. They'd spent the first few hours exploring their designated area, familiarizing themselves with landmarks and the boundaries that they weren't allowed to cross. While he understood the need to be aware of their surroundings, it was beginning to seem as though they'd covered every square inch of their camping area, and then some.

And still, she hiked on, and he dutifully followed, concentrating on the rhythmic sway of her hips and the flex of toned muscles in her smooth, tanned thighs rather than his own body's need to take a rest.

He admitted to being annoyed by her dogged, untiring pursuit at first, but quickly realized that her persistence was a defense mechanism, and her way of showing him that she was in control—of herself and them. After witnessing how thrown she'd been yesterday during their events, and after her request to be alone, he knew she desperately felt the need to grasp a semblance of control over their affair.

For him, though, their affair had crossed the line into a relationship the moment his body had become a part of hers. Their lovemaking had been more honest and real than anything he'd ever experienced with a woman. He couldn't forget the intensity of their joining, and that indescribable moment when she'd given him a glimpse of her deepest desires and emotional needs— when she'd revealed that no one had ever cared about her pleasure before. What they'd shared had been more than hot, gratifying sex, and he suspected she was struggling against that truth. He hoped the next forty-eight hours would forge a deeper intimacy and trust that would last them beyond this one week.

But in the meantime, she was not only pushing his physical limits, she was also determined to up their standing once again by surviving the next two days, and acing the final competition as well. And it appeared she'd do whatever it took to master both.

Little did she know she'd already conquered him, and he was hoping their forced time alone would make her realize that she had nothing to fear from him. He didn't want to take anything away from her, nor demand anything more than she was willing to give. But he did believe there was something between them that went beyond the superficial attraction their fantasy had initiated. Now he just had to convince her of that, too.

Finally, she came to a stop and announced that she'd found the perfect place to pitch the tent—a high, flat, grassy area with a small creek about ten feet away. And not a moment too soon. The first drop of rain landed on the tip of her nose, startling her, as well as causing a frown to form between her brows. Then another splashed on the back of his arm, and within the next fifteen seconds, a steady pattering of rain fell.

He bit back a chuckle and wisely said nothing, knowing she wouldn't appreciate his "I told you so" when she'd allowed her strong will to sway her better judgment. They slipped off their packs and she quickly untied the tent gear from the top of his, then set out the poles, stakes and tarp and went to work constructing what would be their home for the next two days.

The warm rain increased, gradually soaking through

their shirts and shorts and drenching their hair. He
stepped in to assist her, but it quickly became obvious
that he didn't have the first clue as to what he was doing, and he was hindering rather than helping the process, partly because she wasn't forthcoming with in-
structions.

Her bottom lip curled with frustration, and she held
up a hand to ward off his help. "I can do this quicker
and easier on my own."

Immediately recognizing that mutinous glint in her
eyes, he didn't bother arguing and stepped back out of
her way. Since she wasn't familiar with the setup of this
particular tent, it took her longer than normal to con-
struct it. Then she became flustered because he was
watching her, which caused her to fumble even more.
And when she could have used his help to hammer in
the stakes, or adjust the tarp and secure the rain fly, she
didn't ask...and he didn't offer, which upped the tension between them.

Yet another battle of wills ensued, and he let her take
complete charge of the situation. She was trying to push
him away and put distance between them, but he didn't
feel the least bit intimidated by her brusque disposition—not when he knew this was her way of safeguard-
ing her emotions and keeping those barriers of hers as
solidly intact as ever.

The tent gradually took shape into a spacious A-
frame with plenty of width and headroom, and even a
small vestibule to ward off the rain before they slipped
inside the actual living space. Finished erecting their
abode, she tossed their packs inside, crawled in to the
structure, and unrolled the ground cloth, then a foam
sleeping pad. Once that was done, he ducked his head
and entered the tent, too, soaked from head to toe.

So was she, he noticed as his gaze took in the wet, now transparent T-shirt clinging to her full breasts. A sheer, lacy scrap of a bra showed through clearly, as did the tight, puckered tips of her nipples. While the air was humid and warm, there was no denying the rain had cooled their skin. But with every passing second that he spent admiring her lush, responsive body in see-through cotton, heated arousal chased away any lingering chill he felt.

Unceremoniously, and without realizing where his eyes had strayed to, she sat down and untied the laces on her boots. "You might want to take off your boots and socks and the rest of your wet clothing, or else you'll stay damp all night long and get everything else soggy, as well."

She was so serious, diligent, too militant, yet he knew for a fact she harbored a much softer side. Unable to hold back his amusement any longer, he let loose a deep chuckle.

Narrowing her gaze his way, she tugged off a boot and sock, then began working on the other as he plopped down on the comfortable sleeping pad next to her and did the same. "What are you laughing at, Mitchell?"

Undeterred by her prim tone and the use of his full name, he replied very succinctly, *"You."*

Clearly, she found nothing humorous about his answer. "What did I do that you find so funny?" Picking up her boots and socks, she moved on her hands and knees to the tent entrance a few feet away to place her shoes out in the vestibule.

The erratic thrum of the rain against the ground outside matched the unsteady beat of his pulse as he stared at her pert bottom. The wet material of her walking shorts molded to her feminine posterior and elicited thoughts of a very provocative fantasy, of taking her exactly that way, as primitive and wild as the elements around them.

He yanked off his second boot with a low growl and answered her question. "You're just too damned stubborn and headstrong for your own good sometimes."

Reaching for his shoes, she set them next to hers outside then zipped the front closure shut, cocooning them in the sultry warmth and intimacy of the tent that seemed to have shrunk in size. "And that's a problem for you?" she asked, her expression sassy, deliberately provoking.

His *problem* was suddenly their close proximity, the apricot scent lingering in the air, and how in the world he was going to survive the night not touching her. So far, she'd given him no indication that there would be a repeat performance of their love slave fantasy, and he refused to push her into something she wasn't ready for.

Suddenly feeling a bit on edge, and knowing the heightened sexual tension between them was a good part of the reason, he locked his gaze on hers. "Actually, no, it's not a problem for me. I'd think being stubborn and headstrong is more of a problem for *you*."

She visibly bristled. "What's that supposed to mean?"

He exhaled, calling upon a well of patience he knew he possessed somewhere within him. "It means that it wouldn't hurt to give a little sometimes. To let someone else carry a bit of the load once in a while." *To let someone close enough to share fears and burdens and your deepest secrets.* And without questioning why, just knowing that it *was*, he wanted to be that person for her.

Untying her sleeping bag from her pack, she rolled it out with a snap of her wrist. "If you're referring to me letting you help with the tent, it was easier to do it myself."

It was that and many other things between them, and they both knew it. But he played the game her way, in words she'd understand and wouldn't find threatening. "I know I'm not adept at camping and a whole lot of other things when it comes to your lifestyle, but I'm willing to learn if you'd have a little patience and take the time to show me what I need to know."

She settled back on her knees, and he watched the tension ebb from her body. Dragging her fingers through her wet hair to push the damp strands away from her face, she said very softly, very sincerely, "I'm sorry."

"I'm not asking for an apology, Nic, just for you to have a little faith in *me*. All this is new to me," he said of the wilderness event, and fantasies, and them. Gently, he reached out and caressed her jaw with the pad of his thumb. "And I'd really like to make it work, but it's gonna take you meeting me halfway. Do you think you can do that? At least for the next few days?" And he hoped before their time together on Wild Fantasy came to an end he'd find a way to extend that request and coax her to agree to something more long-term than a casual affair.

Her gaze searched his in the darkening tent, the moment becoming a very profound one. There was a tinge of fear in the depth of her velvet green eyes, which was edged out by a sudden strength and yearning that grabbed at something deep and integral inside Mitch.

She nodded, her whole demeanor softening in sweet acquiescence. "Yeah, I can do that."

Relief poured through him. "Good. And now I guess we ought to get out of these wet clothes as you suggested." He stripped off his shirt and tossed it into the corner of the tent for now, figuring that they'd put everything out to dry once the storm passed.

She didn't move, her gaze riveted to his bare chest, and a bolt of desire seared his nerve endings. She was looking at him with such wanting, and a need and hunger he felt all the way down to his bones. Frenzied lightning flashed outside, then was followed by a violent rumble of thunder. Nature found its way inside the tent as well, instigating a restless energy neither one of them could deny. A hot, potent spark flared between them, then sizzled and settled into a slow burn.

"If you don't quit looking at me like you want to eat me up whole, you're gonna end up flat on your back in the next five seconds," Mitch murmured, compelled to warn her of his intent.

"Not if you end up on your back first," she said, and leapt toward him.

Catching him off guard with her abrupt, brazen move, she knocked him flat against his spine, pinning him to the mattress as she scrambled to sit astride his waist. Her expression turned smug and victorious, but there was a playful glint in her eyes that kept the moment light and sexy and flirtatious—and fun. And that was something they both desperately needed after the tension-filled day they'd endured.

She wriggled her bottom against his groin as she shifted on top of him, the friction of their wet clothing eliciting a deep, rumbling groan from his chest. Rolling her to her back would be effortless for him, Mitch knew—just a matter of tipping her sideways and dragging her beneath his hard, very aroused body and taking over from there—but she'd won this round fair and square, and he wanted to see exactly what she had in store for him.

Bracing her hands on either side of his head, she leaned so close her damp hair tickled his jaw, his chest. Her face was flushed, and she smiled at him with tempting, sinful purpose. "I think this time I'm going to make *you* beg for what you want."

Expressing his desires wasn't a problem for him. Not in the least. Neither was begging, if that's what it took to be wrapped in her silky heat again. Tugging her shirt from the waistband of her shorts, he skimmed his hands beneath the hem, touching his fingers to her soft, rain-cooled skin. "I want your clothes off. And mine, too," he rasped.

She sat up straight again, her knees flexing against his sides and her bottom nestling intimately against his erection. "Yes, Master," she said huskily, playing her part as his devoted love slave, as he'd done for her two nights ago.

She brushed his hands away, and he let his arms fall to his sides, deciding that he was going to enjoy watching Nicole strip for him and shed inhibitions in the process. Slowly, provocatively, she peeled her clingy shirt over her head and added the soaked garment to the pile in the corner. With a vixen smile curving her lips, she unhooked her bra, baring her full, lush breasts to his heated gaze. She glided her fingers across the puckered tips and let loose a shudder and moan he felt reverberate through his body as well.

He wanted to touch and taste and be a part of her pleasure. With Herculean effort he restrained from doing any of that, knowing he'd risk shifting the balance of control and shatter this erotic seduction of hers. So, he remained still for now, taking in her movements, graceful despite their cramped quarters, as she stood and slid her shorts and panties over her hips and down her endlessly long legs. She didn't give him much time to admire her gorgeous, naked body before she went to work on his shorts, removing them and his briefs with one quick yank.

"There's a condom in the pocket," he told her before she could toss the pants aside, hoping she'd appreciate that he'd followed through on her request to keep protection handy. And that one was just for starters, since he had more in his backpack.

Her sensual smile told him she was very grateful, indeed. Finding the foil packet and setting it within reaching distance, she knelt between his spread thighs. She leaned over him, and he groaned low and deep in his throat when her lips touched down on his taut belly and her tongue delved and swirled into his navel. Her damp, open mouth was hot on his skin, and her teeth nipped tender flesh as she moved inexorably lower, toward his straining sex. Once there, she encircled him with her fingers, rubbed his shaft against her smooth, cool cheek, and tasted the length of him with a slow lap of her tongue. In typical Nicole fashion, she excited and tormented him, shoving him right to the brink of insanity in less than two fitful heartbeats.

Unable to be a passive participant any longer, he slid his fingers into her hair, knotting the damp strands loosely in his fist. He tugged her head back gently, forcing her to stop her teasing ministrations and look up at him. "Nicole..."

Her compelling dark eyes were filled with heated awareness as she licked the flavor of him from her bottom lip. "I'm not a mind reader, Mitch," she said, using his own words against him. "You're going to have to tell me exactly what you want."

He gritted his teeth as her thumb swept over the head of his penis, a caress that made his entire body jerk in reaction. She was a witch, a sorceress, and he was helpless to resist her charms.

"I want you to take me in your mouth," he uttered, aching to experience the heated textures and sensations of that erotic pleasure with Nicole.

Without hesitation, her mouth enveloped him, taking the length of him in deep, rhythmic strokes. Her wet, silky tongue swirled over the sensitive, swollen tip, sending hot currents of pleasure-pain lancing through him. But it was her own soft, sensuous moan of desire that nearly unraveled his restraint.

He sucked in a sharp breath and swore as his climax beckoned. He wasn't about to let the evening end, not like this, and not without giving to her in return. With his heart pounding as loudly as the driving rain pattering against the tent, he found his voice and tightened his fingers in her hair, pulling her away from him. "Stop, Nic..."

The urgency in his tone captured her attention, and she glanced up at him, her gaze heavy-lidded as she waited to hear his next request.

"C'mere," he murmured, and when she quirked a brow questioningly and didn't move, he gave her what she sought. "I want to taste you, too. *All* of you."

She grinned shamelessly. "All of me, huh? Then that request pretty much covers you for the rest of the night."

He watched her reach for the foil packet next to his hip and tear it open with her teeth. "That's what I was hoping."

With a look of sheer concentration, she sheathed the hard length of him in the snug condom. "And this will cover you for *me*."

And then she kissed her way up his body, gliding her lips over his abdomen, his torso and chest. Straddling his waist, she moved higher. Her feminine heat and damp, downy soft curls brushed across his stomach as she laved his nipples, nuzzled her way to his neck, and whispered naughty things in his ear that made him chuckle, then groan at her boldness. Finally, she bent to take his mouth with her own, drawing him into a long, deep, tongue-tangling kiss that seemed to go on and on....

And then it was his turn to taste and explore, and he did so in the opposite direction, stringing biting kisses along her throat, and down to her breasts. He drew the hardened peak of her nipple into his mouth, then the other, suckling and feasting ravenously on her until she cried out and arched restlessly against him. Knowing what she wanted, and so very in tune with what she needed, he smoothed his palms down her sides and over her slender waist, urging her upward. His lips skimmed her quivering belly, grazed her hip, and her legs widened to accommodate the width of his shoulders as he coaxed her higher still.

The moment his mouth glided across her inner thigh she snapped out of her sensual daze with a startled gasp. Her whole body tensed when she realized exactly what he'd done...and what he planned to do. She clearly wasn't expecting such an erotic position, such a seductive surrender, but much to his relief and pleasure she didn't deny him.

Once her initial shock ebbed, her lashes drifted shut and she let him have his wicked way with her. His mouth was greedy and tender, his tongue hot and un-relenting, unfurling deep and stroking and suckling with insatiable, rapacious hunger. Her breathing deep-ened, her head fell back, and a lusty moan erupted from her throat as the force of her climax sent her soaring.

Before those exquisite contractions had a chance to recede, he grasped her hips and guided her back down the length of his body, impaling her on his throbbing shaft in one smooth, upward thrust. His entry was hard and fast and so deep she inhaled sharply at the heat and pressure of his invasion.

He immediately stilled, cursing himself for taking her with such little finesse and allowing his need for her to overrule common sense. While she was completely primed, she was extremely tight and most likely still very sensitive from her recent orgasm, and he'd plowed into her without thinking about her pleasure.

His pulse pounded furiously at the thought of hurt-ing her in any way—physically, emotionally, it didn't matter, not when she was so much a part of him at this moment that he could feel her heartbeat as strongly as his own. "Nic," he whispered, his own voice aching. "Are you okay?"

A streak of lightning flickered outside, illuminating the inside of the tent and the intimate smile curving her mouth. "I'm better than okay, just a bit...over-whelmed."

He knew the feeling all too well. His gaze snared hers, and there was something in her eyes he couldn't quite decipher, a wistful yearning mingling with a growing urgency. And then it no longer mattered as she sat up straighter, her breath catching again as the action drove him more solidly into her, burying him to the hilt. Splaying her hands on his stomach, she moved her hips in slow, sensuous undulations, arching into him and letting her wild, impetuous side take over.

She flowed around him like hot silk, and he cupped her pale, cool breasts in his hands and flicked his thumbs across the velvet softness of her nipples, arrested by her beauty and passion and irresistible allure. Arrested, too, by the stunning realization that he was falling hopelessly in love with this woman—this fiercely independent woman who refused to believe she needed a man in her life for anything more than a temporary affair.

Feeling the velocity of the storm building, in them and around them, he spread his fingers wide over her rib cage and dragged his thumbs downward, burrowing through hot, moist curls to caress her softly swelled flesh with slow, luxurious strokes that matched the rhythmic glide of her hips. She closed her eyes and let go of a breathless moan that spiraled into a keening cry of pleasure. Her inner muscles clutched him in strong, rippling contractions, and she continued to ride him as she came, as hot and as aggressive as the storm raging outside—as wild as the thunder rumbling across the evening sky—a restless bundle of energy he wanted to capture and keep for his very own.

Her searing climax launched him into his own, a mindless explosion of heat and razor-sharp sensation that tore a low, guttural groan from his chest. When the stunning release was over, she collapsed on top of him and he wrapped his arms around her back and held her close.

He had her body. Now he wanted her heart and soul.

And he only had a handful of days to find a way to lay claim to both.

A LAZY, masculine sigh filled the interior of the tent, a sound of contentment that echoed inside of Nicole. Outside, the worst of the storm had passed, and the light drizzle pattering on the tarp added to the calm serenity present in the wake of the tropical tempest.

Glancing across the foot of space separating her from Mitch, Nicole admired the way the light from their battery-operated lantern cast intriguing shadows over his handsome face and gave a bronze hue to his wide, virile chest. They were both reclining on their sides facing one another, still naked but replete after making love, and completely comfortable in their nudity and with each other in a way that amazed Nicole. The lower halves of their bodies were covered by one of the flannel-lined sleeping bags they'd opened to share as a blanket, and they were picking through a plastic bag of trail mix. He liked the nuts and dried apricots, and her favorites were the raisins and M&M's candies—a perfect exchange that reflected the harmony that had settled between them after a very tension-filled morning and afternoon.

Yes, contentment was most definitely an appropriate word to describe the feeling, Nicole thought with a private smile. She felt a wonderful, rich kind of glow she didn't want to lose. Less than an hour ago she'd allowed herself to give to Mitch with abandon, and he'd taken her to heights of passion she never knew existed. Then again, no man had ever been so focused on her pleasure, her needs, and it was a heady sensation to be the recipient of such all-consuming attention.

But it was more than great sex and multiple orgasms that accounted for the tranquil warmth spilling through her veins. As startling as the knowledge was, it was Mitch himself that contributed to her sense of well-being. His easygoing attitude gave her a sense of stability. And she had to give him credit for his ability to take her shifting moods in stride and even find amusement in her temperament. Then there was his request earlier that they meet halfway, which had melted her resolve to keep him at arm's length.

Even though she knew this particular wild fantasy with Mitch was as temporary as their vacation, she'd come to the conclusion in his arms a little less than an hour ago that it was so much more pleasurable to make love, rather than war, with Mitch. She had to let go a little, and quit fighting him and herself. Especially since the two of them would be spending the next two days and nights in such close confines.

Besides, if the truth were to be told, she liked being with Mitch and enjoyed his company, when she wasn't trying so hard to push him away or grasp the reins of control. So, she was going to take pleasure in this time with him and not question all the other emotions and doubts and insecurities crowding their way to the surface.

Finding a few morsels of dried apricot in the dwindling mix, she fed the pieces of fruit to him. Smiling wickedly, he caught her wrist and nibbled playfully on the tips of her fingers, then licked them clean. "Umm, I could get addicted to this."

She didn't even try to suppress the shiver that raced down her spine and made her skin tingle. "What, being hand-fed trail mix?"

"Definitely that. And making love to you," he murmured huskily, his luminous eyes glimmering with a seductive, golden light. He pressed a very intimate kiss in the palm of her hand she felt all the way to the pit of her belly, then let her go. "And being lazy without a care in the world," he added. "And enjoying myself and not feeling guilty about it."

Ferreting out a red M&M's candy, she popped the chocolate into her mouth and chewed. "What in the world do you have to feel guilty about?"

His smile turned adorably sheepish. "It's self-inflicted guilt, actually, and nobody's fault but my own."

She lifted a brow in interest. "Do tell," she coaxed.

"You already know my father's business became my business when he died, even though I never intended to be an auto broker."

Remembering their conversation from a few days ago, she nodded, and he continued.

"I felt this incredible obligation to make sure my family was taken care of, and I didn't think twice about jumping in and taking over." There wasn't an ounce of resentment in his voice. He'd obviously felt a sense of duty that went hand in hand with familial obligations. "But everything that came with my father's death was incredibly overwhelming. I had so many responsibilities hanging over me, with the business and my family, and I always felt as though taking any time for myself would be like taking extra money away from bills that needed to be paid, family expenses, or college tuition that needed to be doled out. There was always something, and the handful of times I can remember taking a day off I'd worry about how much money I might be losing because I was missing a possible sale."

"Ahh. That's where the self-inflicted guilt comes in," she guessed.

"Yep." He scrounged around for some nuts, tossed her a few plump raisins in the process, then munched on the cashews he'd found. "I was really worried about leaving the business for a week and letting my brother handle things while I took this vacation, but Drew took over so easily that it made me finally see that he's more than capable of running the business without me breathing down his neck. And it also made me realize I've got more freedom now than I've allowed myself since college."

Cool air brushed her skin as nightfall settled in, and she pulled the flannel sleeping bag up around her bare breasts. "Sounds like you spent so much time nurturing everyone else that you didn't nurture yourself."

"That's one way of putting it." He braced his palm against his temple as he reclined on his side, his striking gaze latching on to hers. "Want to know what my fantasy is? The one I put down on my application?"

She hesitated for a heartbeat. She'd never expected their casual conversation to deviate into something so private and personal. Neither did she want him to think she'd divulge her fantasy in return—she wasn't willing to reveal one of her biggest insecurities to him. "Only if you really want to share yours."

He smiled. "It's pretty simple and boring, actually. I wanted to relax, have fun, and enjoy this vacation worry-free."

He didn't pressure her to reciprocate, and she was grateful. "And is your fantasy being fulfilled?"

He blinked lazily, but the sudden heat and desire in his eyes as he stared at her belied his attempt at nonchalance. "Beyond my wildest expectations."

And she was part of the reason, his gaze added silently. A hot, delightful flush coasted down the length of her body at that realization. Still curious to know more, she asked, "Do you regret the choices that you made, doing something that you really hadn't chosen for yourself?"

"No," he replied without a second thought, his tone honest. Rolling to his back, he stacked his palms beneath his head and gazed up at the shadows flickering along the tarp. "I did what I had to do at the time. Now I don't know any differently than the fleet auto business. I enjoy what I do, I'm good at it, and I can't imagine doing anything else." He was quiet for a moment, the soothing sound of the drizzling rain filling the silence before he looked her way and spoke again. "As for those choices, I might not regret the direction my life took, but I am beginning to realize I want more than just work in my life."

She tipped her head curiously. "Such as?"

"I'm thinking my mother might know best after all with her not-so-subtle hints that she wants me to settle down and get married." His voice was low and thoughtful. "When I take work out of the equation, I have nothing but a nice house to come home to—a big, quiet, *empty* house. And lately I've been wondering what it would be like to have someone greet me after a long day at work and give my evenings a little more purpose."

Nicole's chest grew so tight it hurt to breathe—a combination of her own fear of being tied down to one person, and Mitch being tied down to someone else. She frantically sought to grasp a bit of humor to dispel her own strange reaction to his soul-stirring words. "Ever thought of getting a dog?"

He chuckled, the sound sexy and all male. "I was thinking more along the lines of maybe finding myself a wife, having a family of my own and, yeah, maybe a dog, too."

More startling pain, but this time the disturbing ache was centered around her heart, where a lifelong yearning blossomed into something more needy, connected directly to Mitch. She shook off the unexpected tidal wave of emotion that surged through her, tamping it the best she could. He wasn't asking her to be the person he came home to, for goodness sakes—not that she *wanted* to be that woman, she amended quickly.

Not only did she have no desire to be tied down to anything but her business, she knew for a fact from her own past experiences with men, and one in particular, that she could never be the kind of woman Mitch needed in his life. Certainly he needed someone more domesticated, more tame and more demure than herself. Someone who didn't have a sassy mouth and a stubborn attitude and who would live up to a man's expectations of a wife. Someone who wouldn't spend her days and nights on adventures that would take time away from a relationship, she thought, remembering Jonathan's resentful words that had cut deep and left lingering scars.

She and Mitch were good together for a fling, nothing more. That's all either of them wanted or bargained for. And *she'd* do well to remember that.

9

MITCH INHALED a deep breath of crisp, clean air as he followed behind Nicole on the early afternoon trek she'd insisted they take, to pass the time with mild exercise and to appreciate what nature had to offer.

After last night's downpour the morning had dawned bright, warm and beautiful, without a trace of the storm in sight. Much to Mitch's surprise, he'd slept in until nearly nine and woke refreshed and rested to find Nicole outside their tent, dressed for the day and heating water in a small pot on the portable camp stove. She'd greeted him with the kind of sweet smile he could easily become accustomed to seeing every morning, especially after a night of soulful, satisfying sex, and equally meaningful conversation.

As if knowing exactly what he needed to begin his morning, she'd handed him a tin cup of hot, fragrant coffee, then whipped up breakfast for the two of them. While they'd eaten their bland but filling oatmeal they'd chuckled at a pair of squirrels tussling over the leftover nuts Nicole had tossed their way. After cleaning up their campsite and taking care of personal business, they'd set out on their excursion.

So far, Mitch was enjoying everything about their hike—the relaxing, stress-free stroll through easy terrain, their amicable conversation, Nicole's carefree laughter and teasing antics, and even the way she took the time to admire plants and flowers, or stopped him to examine an exotic-looking creature or bug. She loved the outdoors and nature, and through her eyes he discovered a whole different world so vast and varied from the one he'd been living in his entire life. And he liked what he saw inside himself as well as around him—and knew Nicole was the reason for his new sense of awareness.

The warmth of the sun peeking through leaves and branches elevated the level of humidity in the air, and they took a rest near a creek and snacked on the energy bars she'd tucked into her pocket. They spent a good hour sitting there talking about mundane things, as well as likes, dislikes, and more personal, intimate issues in an attempt to ace the final question-and-answer competition—and they discovered they had more in common than either of them realized. They both liked pepperoni-and-mushroom pizza with ice-cold beer, both were fans of old Alfred Hitchcock movies, and they even had similar views on political issues.

During a comfortable lull in their conversation Nicole strolled to the shallow creek and dipped her hands in the crystal-clear water rippling its way downstream. "Wow, it's really getting hot." She passed her wet hands over the loose strands of hair that had escaped her ponytail, then spread the dampness along her throat and arched neck.

He joined her at the creek, finding the temperature of water extremely refreshing. "Maybe you need to cool off a bit more," he said, and playfully flicked a handful of water at her.

She gasped in shock as her T-shirt absorbed the wetness and adhered to her breasts and curves like a second skin. Shooting him a chastising look, she plucked the wet material from her chest, but didn't appear too upset by his behavior. In fact, she suddenly looked downright mischievous. "Now that wasn't very nice, Mitchell."

He chuckled at her strait-laced tone, fairly certain she was planning a payback of her own. "But it had to feel good."

"I'll admit that it did." A tempting smile replaced her admonishing expression as she trailed her fingers in the creek. "But I can think of a few other things that would feel even better."

"Oh, yeah?" he dared, wondering what was going on in that devious little mind of hers. "Like what?"

"Like you and me playing and swimming in that lagoon we passed yesterday that's in our designated area. The one with the waterfall," she said huskily, causing a few erotic fantasies to filter through Mitch's mind.

He glanced around at their surroundings, trying to determine exactly where they were in relation to the lagoon and failing. "I don't remember where it is from here."

Her sultry smile teased him even more. "I do."

He'd be a fool to refuse such a provocative invitation. "Then lead the way, and I'll follow." He moved to stand.

She grabbed his forearm, holding him in place, both of them crouched at the edge of the stream. She tilted her head thoughtfully, causing the end of her ponytail to swipe her shoulder. "What do you say we make this a bit more fun and interesting?"

Recognizing the challenging glint in her dark green eyes, he suspected this was where her brand of sweet retribution came in. "In what way?"

She licked her lips seductively. "If you can find me and catch me, I'm yours to do with as you please."

"Hide-and-seek?" He grinned wryly as he scrubbed a hand along the course stubble on his jaw, which was a result of deciding not to shave for the day. "I already told you I'm not sure where the lagoon is. Are you trying to get me lost?"

Her amused laughter wrapped around him, beguiling and bewitching. "Naww, I wouldn't let that happen and risk you getting us disqualified. Go down that path and I'll leave you a trail of your own to follow," she promised, winking playfully at him. "And just to make sure I get a head start and you don't get overheated while trying to find me, let's cool *you* off a bit."

Before he realized what she meant to do, she gave him a little shove, just enough to throw him off balance and send him sprawling into the creek. His bottom hit the water with an impressive splash, then lapped around his waist and calves, while his shoes remained up on dry ground. He was so taken off guard by her audacity that his jaw went slack. She took advantage of his startled state by tugging on both of his shoelaces, untying them—to slow him down and give her more time to ditch him, no doubt.

With a smug smile, she waggled her fingers at him as she backed toward the trail she'd indicated a few moments ago. "Ta-ta for now, Mitchell."

A low growl rumbled up from his chest, but there was nothing remotely intimidating about the sound. He was enjoying himself and her too much to take any of this seriously. "Get ready to pay and pay dearly!"

She laughed with deep-throated humor, her eyes sparkling with delight. "You have to catch me first," she cajoled, then darted down the path and disappeared from his sight.

He scrambled out of the creek, dripping wet and soggy, but filled with an undeniable charge of excitement. Arousal spiked like a fever in his blood, bringing with it a ripple of sensual anticipation at the thought of capturing Nicole and extracting a final retribution of his own.

He quickly tied his shoelaces, then headed down the same trail she'd taken that took him through a more dense area of foliage. When he came to a fork in the road, true to her word she'd left him a marker indicating what direction she'd gone—her wet T-shirt hung from a low tree branch on the left-hand side of the route.

Grinning, he plucked the article of clothing from its perch and continued on, finding more clues on his way—her lacy bra dangling from a tree limb, her shorts lying on a rock, one shoe, then the other, dropped in the middle of the dirt path. He heard the downpour of the waterfall grow louder as he closed the distance between him and Nicole; the churning sound was as strong as the pulse beating rapidly through his body as he imagined her traipsing through the woods like a nymph.

He found her socks draped on top of a bush, added those to his collection, then spied her silky panties and swiped them up just as he cleared the edge of the lagoon—a breathtaking alcove surrounded by rocks, lush greenery, tropical flowers and a cascade of shimmering water that gave the atmosphere a mystical, magical feel.

But it was the sensual woman completely naked and executing a lazy backstroke in the middle of the pool of water who seized his attention and made him ache with a longing so fierce it nearly brought him to his knees.

She was everything graceful and beautiful—her high, pert breasts crowned with dark, tight nipples, her flat belly, the honey-blond curls between her thighs, and her long-limbed, supple body.

A needful shudder ripped through him. Damn, he wanted her. And he feared the wanting would never end. Feared even more that everything between them would be over before she gave them a firm chance to build something solid and lasting.

She grinned when she caught sight of him, her agile arms continuing their slow backward pedal through the water. "I was beginning to wonder if you'd gotten lost."

"Kind of hard to do when you left me an extremely enticing trail to follow." He dropped her clothes onto a nearby patch of dry grass and toed off his shoes. "You definitely revved up my imagination." And his libido. Oh, yeah, especially that.

"That was the whole point," she replied with characteristic sass as she wriggled her hips and the water undulated over her belly and thighs, mesmerizing him. "You've found me, but you still have to catch me."

With that beckoning taunt, she rolled over onto her stomach in one fluid movement and dove into the depths of the water, leaving him with the very lasting and tantalizing image of her smooth, heart-shaped bottom high in the air, then endlessly long legs that gradually disappeared beneath the surface.

No doubt about it, the woman drove him crazy, upping his adrenaline and tying his emotions in a huge, tangled knot. She also made his blood run hot, and he couldn't rip his clothes off fast enough so he could join her. Once he was stripped bare, he dove into the water without testing it first, finding it cool and refreshing against his feverish skin.

For the next fifteen minutes he chased Nicole, at first playfully and without threat, then gradually his quest grew more serious. True to her Olympic training as a youth, she was a fast, strong swimmer, dodging him with ease and keeping him at a distance while making fun of his futile attempts to apprehend her.

Finally, he worked her into the corner near the waterfall. With her skill and agility, she could have out-swam him with little effort, but there was a certain shameless gleam in her eyes that told him she wanted to be caught.

He advanced toward her, struck with the knowledge that this woman would never, ever bore him. She quickly turned, finding a cluster of rocks behind her and using them to climb the short distance up to the waterfall. Once she was up on the sturdy ledge, she stepped beneath the cascading water, dropping her head back so the downpour washed through her hair, splashed enticingly over her shoulders, and sluiced and trickled its way down her voluptuous body....

Mitch swallowed hard. Untamed desire and ruthless hunger rose in him as he watched her hands skim her slick, wet skin, the feelings swiftly followed by the searing, urgent need to possess and brand her as his woman. His mate. In a way as vital as nature itself.

By the time he'd scaled the rocks to the ledge, she'd disappeared behind the waterfall. Undeterred, he stepped through the shimmering curtain of water and found her standing a few feet away, waiting for him. Her gaze slid down the length of him, lingering on his full, hard erection before traveling upward again. Excitement flared bright in her eyes, and her breathing grew heavy and aroused, and he hadn't even touched her yet.

He inhaled deeply, and his nostrils flared as the moist scents of earth, warm sunshine and damp female flesh assailed him. Everything wild, forbidden and erotic came down to this very moment between them. So did her trust and ultimate surrender. He wanted her, in primitive, carnal ways that would shift the balance of control in his favor this time...if she'd allow it to happen.

He stated his intentions frankly. "In less than thirty seconds I'm gonna catch you, and you *will* be mine," he murmured, "to do with as I please."

She made no attempt to escape as he moved toward her, slowly closing the distance separating them. Neither did she resist him when he turned her around, secured an arm around her slender waist and pressed his naked, fully aroused body against her bottom.

A tremor of response rippled through her, and she reached up and touched her fingers to his stubbled cheek. He nipped the side of her neck with his teeth and soothed the love bites with soft laps of his tongue. A low catch of breath unraveled out of her throat, then coalesced into a soft moan of pleasure when he cupped one of her breasts in his palm and flicked his thumb over her hardened nipple. His other hand traversed downward, sliding between her thighs, stroking through slick, dewy folds of feminine flesh. Male satisfaction expanded his chest when he found her already warm and wet and ready for him.

The cool mist from the waterfall beaded on their skin as he caressed her intimately, deeply, while fondling her breasts. With a gasp, her head rolled back onto his shoulder and her legs buckled, and he took advantage of her pliable body and gently eased her down to her hands and knees on the soft, mossy ground.

Heart pounding, blood thrumming wildly through his veins, he followed her down, his hips and thighs aligned with hers, his chest pressed against her back, his heated breath touching the nape of her neck.

"I want you, Nicole," he whispered raggedly as he kneed her legs farther apart to make room for him in between. His throbbing manhood nestled right at the very heart of her, brushing against the blunt tips of his fingers as he parted her tender, swollen flesh for his possession. "Just like this."

He felt her quiver beneath him. There was no mistaking what he meant, what he intended. And she didn't deny him. "Yes..."

His entire body shuddered with the knowledge of everything she was granting him...not only permission to take her in this provocative, elemental way, but trust—with her body, and her heart as well. They were taking a risk without protection, and he knew Nicole well enough to know she wouldn't allow him this intimacy if he didn't mean as much to her as she did to him.

The emotions that crashed over him with that realization were heady, and with an unraveling groan he flexed his hips against hers, sliding into her with one, smooth penetrating thrust that made her suck in a quick breath and let it out in a rumbling purr of pleasure. He surged again, withdrew, and drove deeper still as the frantic pace increased, forcing a low, animal-like sound he barely recognized from his throat, primitive and purely male.

His teeth grazed her skin, her neck, her cheek, while his fingers plied that sensitive cleft where they joined, making her writhe and moan and beg until he gave her what she sought. He felt her orgasm build with each glide of his fingers, felt her wind tighter with each rhythmic thrust of his hips. Her body strained toward his, until she cried out and came in a pulsing rush of unrestrained ecstasy.

Her wet heat, the arousing scent of her release, and the tight sheath of her body gripping him all went to Mitch's head in a dizzying blitz. With a long, harsh groan, he let go and climaxed right along with her, her name a ragged cry on his lips.

NICOLE PICKED a wildflower on the walk back to their campsite and twirled the stem between her fingers while slanting Mitch a sidelong glance. "I never would have guessed that someone as respectable and stuffy as you would enjoy making love in the middle of nature's finest."

A lazy smile claimed his lips as he scuffed a pebble with the toe of his boot. "Take the boy out of the city and it's amazing how well he'll adapt to the circumstances." Reaching out, he snagged the belt loop on her shorts with a finger and pulled her up against his lean body. His gaze met and held hers. With the backdrop of the dark stubble on his jaw and the equally dark fringe of his lashes, his eyes glowed a much richer shade of brown than normal. "You seemed to enjoy the novelty of our tryst just as much, unless you're used to doing it in the great outdoors?"

His inquiring tone held a playful note, matching the amusing arch of his brow. She could have answered with a reckless, impulsive reply that would have left him wondering, but she was compelled by an inexplicable need to tell the truth. It was suddenly very important to Nicole that he know this brief time with him was becoming a treasured, special memory—beyond any wild fantasy she could have asked for or imagined.

"I guess we're each other's firsts when it comes to outdoor experiences," she admitted, then wriggled out of his embrace and skipped ahead on the trail before he could question her. Before he caught a glimpse into the deepest, most private recesses of her heart and realized that she'd done something incredibly foolish. Before he discovered that she'd fallen hard for him.

She'd always believed that Mitch was the complete opposite of her, and he was, in so many ways. Yet he'd spent the past five days breaching those disparities and showing her just how much they had in common and how well their differences actually complemented one another. Beyond mind-blowing sex and physical attraction there was a mutual tenderness and respect between them she'd never experienced with another man. It was those startling emotions that made her question the loneliness *she* lived with at the end of her adventurous days. And just like other times when she'd been struck with a bout of melancholy, she reminded herself that solitude and being single was a fair trade-off for the freedom and independence she swore was so important to her.

Ignoring the sudden ache blossoming within her chest, she found a distraction and latched on to it. "Look up there, Mitch," she said, pointing to a nearby tree they were passing. "On that second branch between the leaves."

He squinted in the direction of her finger. "It's a lizard."

She laughed, and continued walking backward so she could see and talk to Mitch. "No, it's a chameleon. He's a bluish-green right now, but he can change color and pattern in less than a minute to blend in with the scenery or if he senses danger—'' Her voice wavered as the heel of her shoe caught on a root protruding from the ground, causing her to stumble backward. Her arms flailed as she tried to regain her balance.

Mitch's eyes widened when he realized what was happening, and he automatically leapt forward to grab her and keep her from landing on her butt, but missed latching on to her by an inch. Nicole instinctively threw an arm out behind her to brace herself from the impact of the fall, and her left hand slammed against the hard-packed dirt before her body did, absorbing the brunt of her weight.

She cried out as a stunning bolt of pain darted from her wrist to shoulder. She collapsed onto the ground, seized with excruciating agony, unable to do anything more than roll on her side, cradle her hand to her chest, and moan and choke on the tears gathering in her throat.

In an instant Mitch was on his knees next to her. He didn't touch her, but his mere presence radiated urgency and worry, as did his voice when he barked out his questions. "What's wrong, Nic? Tell me where it hurts."

Paralyzed, rendered speechless by the knife-like pain, the only answer she could utter was a long drawn-out moan that sounded pathetic to her own ears.

His mouth stretched into a grim line, and he skimmed the length of her body with his hands, gingerly searching and probing for broken bones along her legs, hips, ribs, shoulders—completely missing the direct source of throbbing discomfort.

She would have laughed and teased him about his futile attempts if she wasn't in such agony and the situation wasn't so dire. "My...wrist," she told him between panting breaths, and she struggled to a sitting position.

He helped steady her, his gaze latching on to hers. "Is it the same one you shattered in the car accident?"

She nodded jerkily as hot moisture seeped from the corner of her right eye before she could blink it back. She brushed away that bit of vulnerability with a swipe of her good shoulder, hating the helpless feeling swamping her. "Yeah, it's the same wrist."

He swore, the words raw and profane enough to make her wince. He raked his fingers through his still damp, tousled hair, his features fierce and clearly upset. "Can you stand and make it back to our campsite?"

She thought of making a smart-ass comment about her feet not being connected directly to her hand, just to take the edge off her own frustration and anger over her clumsiness, but found she was unable to make a mockery of Mitch's genuine concern. It was her own fault for not watching where she was going and tripping over that root, not his.

She exhaled a choppy breath. "I can make it."

Fifteen minutes later they cleared the trail that led them to their campsite. After sitting her down on a boulder next to the creek, he slipped into the tent and returned in less than thirty seconds with the two-way radio she'd left in her backpack—the one given to them for emergencies.

She jumped up from her seat without thinking, and clenched her jaw when the jarring motion sent a shaft of burning pain racing along her forearm. She remained where she stood, babying her hand, fearful another step would cause another wrenching pang. But that didn't stop her from verbally confronting Mitch. "What are you doing with the radio?"

He stalked over to her, his brows pulled low, his determination palpable. "I'm calling for help," he said succinctly.

A burst of panic swept through her, slamming her heart against her chest in a series of hard beats. Contacting the resort, for any reason, meant forfeiting their place in the competition. And giving up wasn't something she was willing to do, not when they actually had a chance at winning the charity event. *"No."*

His finger stilled on the radio switch, one flick away from turning it on and disqualifying them. "You're as pale as a sheet and obviously in pain," he argued, and glanced at the receiver again.

She also felt light-headed and nauseous, but refused to enlighten him with *that* information. "Don't you *dare* turn that radio on!"

He sent her a dark look, and she stiffened her spine and jutted her chin out defiantly. They stared at each other, wills clashing again. Except this time Nicole was afraid he'd do what he thought was best, regardless of her own wishes, and she'd have to return home and rack up another disappointment.

She remained firm, unbending, unwilling to back down, unwilling to lose to this man in front of her. "Dammit, Mitchell, it's my choice to make, not yours, and I'm not ready to call it quits!"

His eyes flashed hot with irritation. "You might have broken your wrist. *Again.*"

"I'm fine," she lied, hoping and praying it was true.

"You don't know that for certain," he said, jabbing the antennae of the radio her way for emphasis. "And now isn't the time to be stubborn."

"It's a chance I'm willing to take." This time, her tone

brooked no argument. "I can make it until tomorrow morning."

He scowled at her, and she had the fleeting thought that she'd never seen Mitch so angry. Or so fiercely protective. It was the latter that softened something within her, melting away her own temper and replacing her indignation with a remarkable bout of patience.

"I'm not giving up now, Mitch, not when we're so close to making it through this competition," she said, her tone more composed and rational than it had been in the past ten minutes. "And if you so much as turn on that radio, I'll make the rest of your life a living hell," she teased.

The corner of his mouth quirked with a small, wry smile. "Now that's a threat that scares me."

"It should." The fight drained out of her, and she suddenly felt exhausted, emotionally and physically. "Please, Mitch," she said softly, imploringly, "let me try to get through tonight."

His tense shoulders relaxed, contradicting the narrowing of his gaze and the shake of a long finger near her face. "I swear, you are the most hardheaded woman I know. And I'm telling you right now that I don't agree with what you're doing—"

She held up her good hand to ward off his tirade, relieved that she'd managed to sway him. "You don't have to agree or even understand. But I'd really appreciate it if you could help me splint my wrist with something."

He stared at her for a long moment, then shook his head. "I can tell I'm not going to win this one, no matter how hard I try. You sit right here by the creek, and I'll see what I can find to use as a makeshift splint. And it wouldn't hurt for you to keep your hand in the cool water to help with any excess swelling."

She touched his arm, wanting to express her gratitude. "Thank you." The words seemed so simple and inadequate in contrast to what he was giving up for her—his own responsible, conscientious principles.

"You're welcome," he said, his tone taut with resignation. He walked away, grumbling beneath his breath about her mulish attitude and why he even bothered to put up with her. He tossed the radio back inside the tent, then went in search of something long, flat and sturdy enough to immobilize her wrist.

Ten minutes later he returned, his mood improved, looking extremely pleased with himself and his find—a thin piece of rigid bark from a tree. He knelt next to where she sat, withdrew her hand from the cool water, and gently examined her arm and wrist. She winced and gritted her teeth a few times as he probed a particularly painful area.

With infinite tenderness, he ran his fingers along the framework of bones from her wrist down to her palm. "Nothing feels broken."

"My hand is actually starting to feel much better," she said, injecting a bright, cheerful note to her voice.

He shot her a skeptical look that clearly stated he believed she was telling him a tale.

She rolled her eyes, which he didn't see since he'd refocused his attention on her injury. "I know the general area is swollen and still painful, but I can flex my fingers a little bit." She did so for his benefit, and managed not to flinch or groan in agony. "I'm betting it's a sprain."

"Regardless, we still need to immobilize it until we can get a doctor to confirm that nothing is fractured or broken, especially since you've shattered this wrist before."

Resting her hand on her knee for a minute, he pulled off his T-shirt and ripped a small hole in the soft material with his teeth. He tore the garment into long strips that he wrapped tight around her arm before bracing the rough piece of bark along her wrist and palm, then used the excess cloth to cover and secure the splint with ties.

She watched him doctor her up, amazed by his efficiency, while her heart swelled with gratitude at how careful he was not to hurt her or cause her more pain. His head was bent, tossing his sable hair across his forehead, and his expression was etched with intense concentration. An indescribable longing welled up in her, so acute it touched her soul. It made her ache for things she had no business wishing for with a man who needed more than she could ever give him.

Finished with his task, he sat back on his heels and looked up at her. "There, that ought to do it for tonight."

She checked out his handiwork, impressed with his improvisation. "You're very resourceful. I like that in a man." She waggled her brows playfully, doing her best to lighten the mood between them and chase away her own emotional thoughts.

Her teasing brought a smile to his lips, but something more serious lingered in the depth of his eyes. "Tell me something, Nic. Why is winning this competition so important to you? I mean, look at the lengths you're willing to go to," he said, gesturing at her wrist.

She waved her good hand in the air, dismissing his question. "I told you, I'm fine."

"And you just might be," he agreed, sounding more

optimistic than he had before he'd splinted her wrist. "But humor me, quit being so evasive and answer my question."

She affected a blasé look. "Trust me, it's a long and boring story."

"I do trust you. And we've got a good eighteen hours ahead of us which is a lot of time to talk about a whole lot of stuff, and you've yet to bore me this past week. In fact, I've come to the conclusion that you boring me is an impossibility." He stood and motioned her over to their campsite. "Come over here and sit down by the tent while I make us some stew for dinner, and you can talk my ear off."

"I'll help with dinner."

He shook his head and leaned inside the tent to grab one of the sleeping bags, then spread it out for her to sit on. "No, you'll sit and watch, and talk."

"I still have one good hand, ya know," she retorted sassily.

"Save it for later and I'll put it to good use." Grabbing her uninjured wrist, and careful not to jostle her bandaged one, he pressed a soft, damp kiss in her palm, then flattened her hand on his bare, warm chest, right over his heart, which beat steady and strong. "Do you realize it's okay to depend on someone when you need help? It won't take anything away from the strong, independent woman you are."

His words were filled with such conviction, but she'd spent a lifetime struggling to be self-reliant and free-thinking, certain relying on anyone for anything would make her the kind of weak, needy female who'd bend and conform to her parents' wishes.

"I'm not used to someone taking care of me," she admitted.

"No, you're too busy being stubborn and bossy and trying to stay in control of yourself and everything around you." He softened his comment with a brush of his lips across her forehead. When he looked at her again, his eyes gleamed with tenacity, but affection, too. "Tonight, *I'm* in charge, and if you don't like it, you're welcome to return to the resort."

Which they both knew she wouldn't do. He was pushing her hottest buttons, and with anyone else she would have been indignant and flatly refused to give in to his take-charge attitude. But there was something about Mitch that made her want to share with him. Maybe it was the fact that he'd been so open and honest with her this week about his own past. Maybe it was the fact that she wanted him to understand her drive and ambitions and where it all stemmed from. Or maybe it was just the man himself that made her feel comfortable enough to share her own personal insecurities without the fear of being judged or ridiculed.

Whatever the reason, she knew she wouldn't deny him.

"I guess you've given me no choice." She moved out of his embrace and sat down on the soft, flannel sleeping bag. "Okay, I'll sit and watch you make our dinner...and talk."

10

WHY IS WINNING *this competition so important to you?* A simple question with a very complicated answer. So, she started at the beginning.

"When I was born, I wasn't quite what my father was hoping for," she began, watching as Mitch hooked up the small camp stove with more proficiency than she would have given him credit for. "My dad wanted a boy, and he got one two years later when Robert came along."

Mitch finished attaching the butane to the burner, ignited the fire, then glanced up at her. "I thought all little girls were supposed to be the twinkle in their father's eye."

She could well imagine that adorable twinkle in Mitch's eye when and if he ever had a baby girl of his own. She also knew instinctively he wasn't the kind of man who would play favorites with his children.

"Not in my parents' household." Crossing her legs, she cradled her wrapped arm in the crook of her opposite elbow, grateful for the conversation that took her mind off the throbbing ache in her wrist. "Even as a toddler I can remember how much more attention my father gave Robert over me. Robert was the first one he wanted to see when he came home from work, and I ended up with an obligatory pat on the head. He'd take him golfing on the weekends and to the park to play ball while I stayed home with my mom. He never asked if I wanted to go with them, and when I'd beg him to let me come along he'd tell me that they were doing boy stuff and little girls didn't play ball and get their hands and dresses dirty."

"So, I take it you did just that." Amusement danced in his eyes as he used a Swiss army knife to cut open their pouch of stew.

"It did get my father's attention, and even though it was in the form of disapproval, it was more attention than I ever had before from him. Around the time I turned eight I rebelled, big-time. I decided that I hated the frilly dresses my mother bought for me and would sneak into my brother's room and take his shirts and jeans to wear. And I especially refused to be a sweet, quiet girl who was expected to be seen, but not heard."

His laugh was deep and hearty. "Oh, boy. Sounds like mutiny."

She grinned, able to see the humor in her story, yet knowing her father's actions, and her own, had shaped her into the headstrong woman she'd become. "Yeah, I guess it was my own way of putting up a protest. From then on, everything my brother did, I did, too. Except my main goal was to be better than him, in every way."

He dumped the thick beef stew into a pot and placed it over the burner. "Ah, that's where that competitive nature of yours comes in."

She shrugged, not ashamed to admit that truth. "As it turned out, not only did I like sports, but I was good at them. Better than my brother ever was. I played softball and soccer, but I loved swimming the most, and that was something my brother hated. During the summers I'd spend hours at the community pool, and it was there that a swimming coach saw my potential and started working with me. Before long, he had me hooked up with another coach and I was training for the Olympics, and you know how *that* story ended."

He listened, waiting for her to continue, stirring the bubbling contents of the pot. The rich, savory aroma wafted her way, and her stomach growled, making her realize she was hungrier than she'd originally thought.

"I think a part of me knew that I was doing it more for my father than myself. In this one area he really took an interest in *me* and what I was doing. My father would come to my meets and competitions, encourage me to try harder, to win a medal...." Her voice trailed off, and she plucked at a piece of lint on the soft flannel. "It was wonderful having him all to myself for a change and being the center of his attention. Of course after my accident and I was replaced on the team he lost interest again."

She rolled her stiff shoulders and went on without thinking. "And then I met Jonathan, and both my father and mother were thrilled that I'd found such a catch. He came from a prominent family, was an up-and-coming city councilman, and my parents encouraged his interest in me." She watched Mitch spoon the stew into two individual tin bowls, but judging by the way his gaze strayed to her face in between scoops, she'd most definitely captured his interest with her new topic. "We were together for about a year and, surprisingly, my relationship with Jonathan lasted longer than any I'd ever had."

Mitch tipped his head curiously. "How do you mean?"

"Most of my relationships with men have been very short-lived," she said, surprised at the ease in which she was able to admit one of her greatest insecurities out loud. "It started in high school actually. I'd get asked out on a date, but as soon as the guy realized how sports-oriented and competitive I was, they'd feel intimidated by me and would end up breaking things off. I had a lot of guy *friends*, and it just seemed easier, and less painful emotionally, to keep things that way."

"They were boys, Nicole. Of course they were going to feel threatened by a girl who was better at sports than they were." Mitch came over to her and gently maneuvered her arm out of the way while he tucked the corner of the sleeping bag into the crook of her crossed legs, then secured the bowl of stew in the padded lining for her.

"Most men are the same way," she refuted, speaking from personal experience. She pushed her spoon through the thick, steaming stew as Mitch settled beside her with his own dinner. "Especially if they don't like what I do for a living, or feel uneasy about not being able to keep up with me on an outdoor adventure."

"Was Jonathan threatened by your abilities?"

"He refused to accompany me on any trips and told me that roughing it wasn't his idea of fun." She took a small bite of savory beef and potato, and swallowed the surprisingly tasty stew. "I'd say he resented the time I devoted to All Seasons more than anything else. Like my father, and others, Jonathan didn't approve of my business with Guy and had certain expectations of me I knew I could never live up to. It was a mutual decision to break up, but I know my father holds me responsible for giving up such a solid marriage prospect."

"Obviously, you didn't love him."

"No, I didn't," she said quietly, honestly. "We had different ideals, and if we'd gotten married, we would have made each other miserable. Luckily for my parents, my brother came through for them. He's on his way to becoming a successful orthopedic specialist, is married to a very traditional, sweet woman, and they have a baby due soon." She ate another bite of stew and flashed a grin his way to keep the mood upbeat, despite the feelings of inadequacy that hung over her. "That kinda takes some of the pressure off me. For now, anyway."

A thoughtful, "Mmm," was his only reply.

By the time they finished their dinner and Mitch had cleaned up, twilight had moved in, bringing with it a slight chill in the air. The chirp of crickets and other night sounds echoed in the distance. He retrieved the other sleeping bag from the tent and opened it to use as a blanket.

"What's that for?"

"It's such a clear night I thought maybe we could stay out here for a while." He removed his boots, then stretched out on his side next to her. "The stars are so bright and beautiful."

She gazed upward, taking in the glittering lights, the sky a backdrop of black velvet. "Yeah, they are."

"I've never spent an evening outdoors, and I figure there will never be a better time for another first than tonight." He patted the sleeping bag next to him. "Come here and lie next to me, Nic."

Unable to refuse him anything, especially not the opportunity to be close to him, she toed off her shoes, too, then carefully settled against his left side as he pulled the flannel cover up to their waists. His arm slid beneath her neck, and she rested her head on his shoulder and draped her splinted hand across his belly, out of harm's way. The dull ache in her wrist did nothing to detract from the warmth and contentment unfurling within her.

A few minutes later, realizing that Mitch wasn't stargazing but was staring at her instead, she met his golden brown eyes. "Um, you're not looking at the stars."

His shoulder lifted in a shrug. "What can I say, I'm distracted by something much more beautiful."

And with him, she did feel beautiful, and desirable— like a woman who was the center of a man's devotion, caring, and sensual cravings. It was a novel feeling, one she'd enjoy while it lasted. "Flattery will get you everywhere, Mitchell."

"That's what I'm hoping, sweetheart." His grin was pure sin, making her pulse quicken. "But first, do you realize that you never answered my question?"

She frowned. "Which was?"

He shifted slightly, making them both more comfortable. "Why is winning this competition so important to you?"

She groaned. "Are we back to that?"

"Yeah, we are." He ran the tip of his finger down the slope of her nose. "As much as I wanted to hear about your past, and your father, and even Jonathan, all of which have given me a whole new understanding of you, I'd like an answer to my original question. And just as soon as we air that issue, I'd be happy to be your love slave tonight and fulfill your deepest, most secret fantasies." He followed that up with a sexy wink.

Little did he know, he'd already given her more than she'd ever dreamed possible. Beyond fulfilling any and every wild fantasy she'd ever imagined, he'd filled her soul—with laughter and passion and emotions that frightened her on so many levels. And in two days, they'd go their separate ways again, as they'd agreed. As she knew was best for both of them.

Regardless of that painful knowledge, she'd be crazy to refuse one more night of ecstasy in his arms. "You drive a hard bargain, Mitchell."

He chuckled. "Whatever works. Now fess up."

She averted her gaze, staring up at the night sky and finding the Little Dipper in the distance. "I don't want to let my mother down, who is expecting us to win for her charity," she said, stating the obvious. Then she dug a little deeper for more courage and honesty. "And for once, *just once*, I'd really like to have my father's approval and respect, rather than more disappointment or criticism."

Mitch leaned over her, and with his fingers he tipped her chin toward him, so she had no choice but to look directly at his face and see the shadows of understanding and wisdom etching his features. "Maybe winning this charity event is something you need to do for nobody but *yourself*."

Her written fantasy came back to her in a rush: *win or lose, she wanted to be appreciated for who she was and not for what she accomplished.* Yet winning *had been* her sole focus, to the extent that she'd lost sight of her own fantasy. Despite everything, she was still seeking her father's approval, his unconditional acceptance.

Confusion assailed her, making her dizzy from all the jumbled thoughts whirling through her mind. She wasn't sure what was important to her anymore. So many things had changed for her this week—her purpose for being on Wild Fantasy and, most especially, what she wanted for herself, her new desires embodying exactly what she'd swore she didn't need in her life.

A sudden desperation squeezed her chest tight, making her feel as though she was going to lose something very important once this charity event was over. Something more precious than her independence or her father's approval. She stood to lose this sensitive, caring man she'd fallen in love with.

Her breath caught as she finally put a name to the emotion that had been clawing its way to the surface for the past few days. She was stunned and completely, totally awed by the revelation. She was in love with Mitch.

Fearful of such a deep, abiding emotion, she sought to distract her heart and mind. With her good hand, she reached up, curled her fingers around the nape of his neck, and brought his mouth down to hers, telling him with her bold, intimate kiss what she wanted and needed from him—to be cherished and adored one last time. And this time, he didn't ask her to verbalize her desires. They communicated with their bodies, eager touches and uninhibited caresses, and deep, soulful kisses.

He helped strip off her shirt, shorts and underwear, then undressed himself quickly, and that brief separation made her burn even more for him. He returned, pressing her back on the soft flannel while taking infinite care to make sure her wrist didn't get jostled, and pulled the covers up around them.

Her thighs parted, making room for him in between. Feverish gazes locked, and he moved over her and in her with one long, slow thrust that made them both moan with the pleasure of their joining. No foreplay or preliminaries were necessary for either one of them. They were both ready for the ride, and she lifted her knees, wrapping her legs high around his waist as they easily found the personal rhythm that was uniquely theirs.

He touched her in ways she had no idea a woman could be touched. Inside, outside and everywhere in between. She was spellbound and enthralled. For so many years she'd denied that she had needs. Denied her yearning to belong to one special person.

She denied herself nothing now.

With the trembling fingers of her good hand, she touched Mitch's roughened cheek and stared deeply into his eyes. *Love me,* she thought. *Just the way I am, with all my flaws, imperfections and insecurities. Love me...just for tonight.*

As if he had a direct source into her mind and thoughts, he did just that. He made love to her body and soul, giving her pleasure and passion and demanding absolutely nothing in return. Gradually, she felt the shift of emotion between them, saw the hope of forever glow in his breathtaking eyes, and was frightened by what she'd witnessed...and so very afraid that she'd never be able to live up to Mitch's expectations and needs. Which didn't include a stubborn, headstrong, independent woman more intent on being alone than relying on another person for anything....

Tonight, he didn't allow her to retreat or wallow in fears or doubts. No, she figured there would be plenty of time for all that later, like tomorrow.

Seemingly knowing her better than she knew herself, he dipped his head and distracted her with a deep, thorough kiss that elicited a greater hunger. Heat rippled beneath her skin, and she moved restlessly beneath him, with him, moaning softly as her pulse quickened and her release built to a crescendo. He arched against her one last time, high and hard, sending her soaring up to the heavens in a shuddering climax.

She cherished the moment, the memory, and the man who made it all possible, holding all three safe, secure and close to her heart...just as Mitch held her close to his all through the night.

"WHAT'S TAKING so damn long?" Mitch growled beneath his breath.

Frustrated and agitated, he scrubbed his fingers through his freshly showered hair as he paced the length of the small waiting room. Nicole had left him there nearly an hour ago to see the resort's doctor after insisting on going into the patient room alone. After everything they'd shared the past few days, having her shut him out that way irked the hell out of him.

He inhaled a deep breath, which did nothing to calm the emotional upheaval within him. They'd returned from their wilderness survival event having qualified for the final round question-and-answer session, along with three other teams. Two of the couples had dropped out of the competition because they'd been unable to handle the unsophisticated living arrangements and rough elements for two days, and another team had to forfeit their place when one of them had gotten bitten by a spider and suffered a severe allergic reaction.

The four final teams had been given two hours to change and rest before participating in the last event that would determine the winners of the three top monetary prizes. While Mitch had suggested to Nicole that they see the doctor for her wrist immediately, she'd insisted on a shower and a fresh change of clothes first. Having learned it was useless to argue with her when

she was so single-minded about something, he'd be-
grudgingly let her have her way, then met up with her
at the doctor's office—only to be left out in the waiting
room to worry and wonder what was going on behind
that closed door.

Mitch should have known the instant she'd woken
up that morning, having reverted back to Ms. Independent, I-can-make-it-back-to-the-resort-on-my-own-just-
fine, despite her still swollen and painful wrist, that
something was very wrong. He'd grown used to dealing with her sassy mouth and attitude, and she'd been
way too quiet for his peace of mind on the trek back to
the resort. He didn't believe her silence and distant demeanor had anything to do with her injury bothering
her as she claimed. No, the cause was what had transpired between them last night. He'd felt the incredible
closeness when they'd made love, the intimacy and
bond they'd created together.

He'd also seen her panic and felt her attempt to retreat when the moment became deeply emotional. He'd
tried his damnedest to make her realize that she had absolutely nothing to fear from him—even going so far as
to hold back the words that had nearly slipped from his
lips when he'd been deep, deep inside her.

I love you. A life-altering declaration he'd never given
another woman, and a heart-and-soul commitment he
was willing to make to Nicole. Unfortunately, he didn't
think she was in the frame of mind to appreciate his gift,
or even accept it. Her barriers were back up, stronger
and more impenetrable than before. She was running
scared of what was between them, and fearful of how
quickly their relationship had evolved into something
more meaningful than a love-slave fantasy. He was just
plain scared that he was going to lose Nicole before he

really ever had her. And pushing her to make a decision, or demanding more than just this one week together, would only make her rebel and withdraw further, he knew.

At a loss as to what to do, he stopped his pacing and dropped into a nearby chair. He cradled his head in his hands, feeling as though he'd been sucked through an emotional whirlwind in the past twenty-four hours—hell, since this whole fantasy business had begun, actually. He'd come to the island for rest, relaxation and fun, and instead had discovered what had been missing from his one-dimensional, streamlined life—one special person to share it with. Nicole. A sexy-as-hell woman who made him enjoy life. An impulsive woman who kept him guessing. A smart-mouthed, reckless woman who made every moment of every day interesting and most definitely an adventure. And beneath all those other complex layers she wore like armor he'd unearthed a vulnerable, sensitive woman who needed his love as much as he craved hers in return.

Cynical laughter sputtered out of him. "Like she'd ever admit to needing anything from *me*," he muttered.

Another ten minutes and the door to the patient rooms finally opened and Nicole stepped out. Mitch jumped up from his seat, his gaze traveling from the cast on her left arm to her reserved expression.

He ached to touch her, but was no longer certain where he stood with her so he kept his hands to himself. "Is everything okay?"

She lifted her arm up to give him a better look at the fresh cast. "As okay as things can be with a fractured wrist."

He winced at the painful thought, grateful, at least,

that they'd splinted her injury last night. "Aw, Nic, I'm sorry. How long do you have to wear the cast?"

She shrugged nonchalantly, brushing off his sympathy. "The doctor said four to six weeks and it should be good as new, but I'll consult my physician, too, when I get back home. In the meantime, it looks like I'll be riding a desk at work for a while." Her voice was flat, devoid of any real emotion. She slanted a glance at the clock on the wall and smoothly changed the subject. "If we don't hustle we're going to miss the last round of competition."

He jammed his hands on his hips and stared at her as a fresh surge of frustration rose within him. The competition. Of course that would be *her* main concern. Right now, at this very moment, he could give a rip about the final contest.

But it was important to her. That much he knew and understood.

"You're right," he said, his irritable tone openly expressing his increasingly bad mood. Grasping her good elbow, he ushered her toward the exit. "We have a charity event to win."

And if she wouldn't take anything else from him, he could at least do his best to ensure a first-place win that would give her the approval and respect she sought so badly from her father.

"WHAT IS YOUR partner's favorite color?" Merrilee's assistant, Danielle, asked the contestants who were part of the four teams left in the final event, which included Penny and Graham.

Nicole jotted down what she knew would be Mitch's answer on the small piece of poster board everyone had been supplied with for the question-and-answer session. She bit her bottom lip as a memory swamped her, of her and Mitch playing in the lagoon after making love beneath the waterfall. He'd caught her up in his arms, gazed deeply into her eyes, and informed her that he loved the vibrant green hue of her irises and that would always be his favorite color. In a moment of sharing she'd revealed hers in return, red, and he'd teased her that it suited her personality. Racy, impulsive and sexy.

Taking a steady breath, she set her pen down to indicate she was ready and glanced across the ten feet of space that separated the men contestants from the women—and met Mitch's intense, probing stare. He'd answered the question, too, and while they waited for the others to finish as well, his gaze brought up a dozen silent, personal issues—the most prominent of which was *why was she putting distance between them after such an incredible week together?*

The answer was complicated, in some ways even for her to understand. She'd spent so many years struggling to be self-sufficient and in charge of her emotions after a very turbulent childhood and disastrous breakup with Jonathan, and within the span of a few days she'd lost complete control with Mitch—physically, mentally and emotionally. In her wildest dreams she never could have imagined that their affair would make her yearn for so much more, things she swore she didn't need in her life.

She'd always feared letting anyone as close as she'd allowed Mitch, and now she knew why. She was afraid of not being the kind of woman he needed in his stable, responsible life. She was wild and free and at times openly rebellious. He was rock solid, grounded and rational to a fault. She relished the outdoors, risky adventures, and he was far more cautious. Take away the incredible physical aspect of their relationship and the two of them just didn't mix. Not long-term, anyway, as she'd learned from her own personal experience with prominent, respectable Jonathan.

In a desperate act to protect what was left of her heart, and not wanting to hurt Mitch in the long run, this morning she'd started the painful process of rebuilding those barriers that would keep him at an emotional distance. He was clearly upset at her withdrawal, but in another day they'd return to Colorado, their own individual and different lives, and he'd realize that she'd done them both a huge favor.

But before they left the island, before they parted ways, they had a charity event to win for their mothers, and she still had her own personal fantasy to fulfill. She hoped that claiming victory in this final round of competition would grant her what she ultimately sought— that acceptance and approval she'd craved since childhood.

While she and Mitch correctly guessed each other's favorite color, along with two other couples, one team obviously hadn't discussed that individual preference and were eliminated. They were down to three teams, all of whom were assured a monetary prize, the amount depending on where they placed in this final round.

Penny, who was sitting next to Nicole, fidgeted anxiously in her seat as they awaited the next question. Nicole smiled encouragingly at the other woman when she glanced her way and received a glimpse of just how nervous and hopeful Penny was.

Danielle posed the next question, pulling Nicole's thoughts back to the competition. "How many siblings does your partner have?"

An easy answer for her and Mitch, and one they aced. Everyone else on the panel replied correctly, too, obviously having discussed family ties in some regard.

"What is your partner's favorite food?" Danielle asked once the applause from the guests died down.

A tough one for most, but another recollection filtered through Nicole's mind, of lying in Mitch's arms the night of the storm. Her stomach had growled hungrily because they'd skipped dinner, and he'd playfully asked if she could choose anything at all to eat in that moment, other than the bland fare they'd been given for the camping trip, what would it be? She'd selected lasagna, and he'd picked his mother's chicken potpie.

It might not be their top favorite food, but it was all either one of them had to go on, and enough for both of them to win the round with their matching answers. The third couple bombed on the question, while Penny and Graham managed to guess accurately, too. With one hundred thousand dollars and her brother's upcoming surgery costs at stake, Nicole suspected Penny and Graham had spent the past two days preparing themselves for any and all types of questions in their quest to capture the grand prize. So far, her and Mitch's answers were matching on coincidence and pure luck.

Danielle flipped to the next index card in her hand. "What is your partner's favorite type of music?"

Nicole picked up her pen and wrote down "country" on her card for Mitch's answer, recalling a conversation she had with Mitch during their hike about how he and his brother were constantly jockeying over the radio station in the office—him for country, and his brother for New Age. She'd teased Mitch about how opposite they were in their tastes, and told him she preferred rock 'n' roll.

A soft, strangled sound from Penny's throat caught Nicole's attention, and she cast a surreptitious and concerned glance at the other woman. Penny's expression was panicked, her eyes filled with despair as she stared across the room at Graham, who sat calm and composed and seemed to silently urge his teammate to do her best and take the best educated guess she could. Penny closed her eyes, inhaled a steady breath, then picked up her pen and wrote down an answer. There was no doubt in Nicole's mind that Penny's reply was a shot in the dark.

Nicole was hit with the fleeting, somewhat disturbing thought that Penny was going to lose to her and Mitch. Her stomach twisted with regret, and in that moment she wished she had the power to change the outcome of this contest—in Penny's favor. Here was a person in desperate need of that prize money, for a truly worthy, admirable purpose—to help save her brother's life. While there was no denying her mother's organization was just as deserving, Nicole realized belatedly that she was being competitive for all the wrong reasons. Selfish reasons, in comparison to Penny's motivations.

Danielle asked for her and Mitch to present their answers, and they both made a match. In private agony, Nicole watched as Penny tentatively announced her preference of music out loud—rock 'n' roll—and Graham quickly and with obvious enthusiasm lifted his card to reveal those same words written on his card. Then it was Graham's turn to state his answer, and he went with the same reply as hers, his uncertain tone of voice telling the audience he was making a guess, as well. Penny cried out in relief and delight as she flipped her card over, revealing matching answers.

Their two teams remained at a stalemate.

Nicole blinked in unexpected shock, which was quickly replaced with a rush of gratitude. By sheer luck or divine intervention—she didn't care which was responsible—she'd just been granted the private wish she'd made minutes ago. Penny's intentions were so incredibly selfless, based on love and devotion. While Nicole envied that unconditional affection, she respected it more, and she wasn't about to give up the opportunity to grant a very special person the chance to relieve a huge financial medical burden and make her brother's future a bit brighter.

But first, she and Mitch had to lose.

Once the excitement buzzing through the crowd settled down, Danielle cleared her throat and read another question. "Which does your partner prefer as a pet. A dog or a cat?"

Nicole bit back a groan. She'd been hoping for a question that they didn't know the answer to that would cause them to lose legitimately. Earlier in the week Mitch had mentioned during casual conversation that his mother was taking care of his house cat while he was on vacation, and she'd told him the only animal she'd ever consider getting for herself was a Golden Retriever.

Chewing on her bottom lip uncertainly, she looked across the room at Mitch as he wrote down his answer, turned his card over, then lifted his gaze to hers and gave her a small, private wink that said they'd definitely win this round. She glanced at her competitors. The huge smile on Penny's face, coupled with the victorious gleam in Graham's eyes told Nicole the other couple knew each other's answers. Torn as to what she should do, she jotted down the answer on her card, and the session resumed.

Penny and Graham went first this time, their excitement tangible when their answers matched. Mitch called out "cat" for his reply, which matched Nicole's guess. Then it was Nicole's turn to reveal her preference. Her heart pounded erratically in her chest, echoing loudly in her ears, and her right palm grew clammy as everyone waited for her to state her answer. Knowing she couldn't count on Penny and Graham winning the next round, she came to the conclusion that she had no choice but to throw the competition *now*. Pushing aside any misgivings and doubts, she spoke loudly, "Cat."

Mitch's jaw dropped and he stared at her in disbelief as he slowly turned his card over, revealing the correct answer of "dog," making Penny and Graham the first-place winners of the charity event. The other couple whooped and hollered in supreme joy, and the guests joined in on the noise by whistling and clapping wildly. Nicole looked away from Mitch's still stunned expression and stood, taking the few steps toward Penny to congratulate her on winning the one-hundred-thousand-dollar grand prize.

The other woman pulled her into an exuberant hug, and Nicole returned the embrace, wincing as her still tender wrist and awkward cast got bumped in the process.

"Congratulations, Penny," Nicole said once the other woman let her go. "Your family is going to be so proud of you."

"Thank you, Nicole." Penny beamed from the compliment. "My brother means the world to me, and this money will help so much with his heart transplant."

"I know." Nicole smiled softly. "He's extremely lucky to have you for a sister."

Penny's happiness was infectious, infusing Nicole with a jolt of rightness and a deep sense of pride. Deliberately losing the charity event was the most difficult, yet surprisingly easy and liberating decision of her life. But she harbored no illusions that the aftermath of her decision would be incredibly painful and extremely emotional. Starting with Mitch. And she only had a handful of seconds before he made his way across the crowded room and confronted her with what she'd done.

Nicole touched the other woman's arm, making sure she had her attention once again before she followed through on one of her most rebellious decisions yet. "Penny...I'd like to donate my half of my second-place winnings to your brother's trust."

Penny gasped in surprise. "Oh, Nicole..." Tears of gratitude filled her eyes and overflowed when she blinked. "That's incredibly generous...I don't know what to say."

"There's nothing to say," she replied genuinely. "I want to do it, and I'll make arrangements with Merrilee to make sure the twenty-five thousand dollars gets transferred to your brother's trust."

Graham arrived, interrupting the two of them with his boisterous, "We did it!" Then he swept Penny up into his arms and twirled her around.

Nicole's head began to pound—from the crush of people suddenly swarming around them, from her aching wrist, and from the thought of what still lay ahead for her. Taking advantage of the distraction to make an escape, she turned and literally bumped into Mitch. So much for slipping out unnoticed, or avoiding an interrogation. She stepped back and glanced up, and her stomach bottomed out at the fierce frown lining his features and frustration glittering in his dark eyes.

He crossed his arms over his chest, looking way too formidable and determined. "Care to explain what's going on?" he demanded.

She straightened her spine in defense. "I'm not sure I know what you mean."

His jaw worked, and his gaze narrowed. "You know damn well what I mean," he said, his tone low and precise. "You sabotaged that last question, Nicole. We had every chance at winning and you deliberately lost the competition. I don't get it."

Her throat tightened, and she realized that tears were the culprit. She'd let Mitch down, that much was obvious. She felt conflicted inside, her heart torn in two different directions. Mitch's opinion of her mattered more than she'd ever anticipated, and she wasn't sure he'd understand her personal reasons for losing the competition when that had been their sole purpose of being at the island resort.

"I'm sorry, Mitch." It was the only answer she could give him for now. The emotional upheaval clamoring within her was wearing her down, the tears in her throat now burning the backs of her eyes. Swallowing hard and praying for a few more seconds of composure, she pressed her fingers to her forehead. "I'm not feeling real well. Would you do me a huge favor and please stay for the reception and accept the second-place prize for both of us?" Not giving him a chance to refuse her request, she darted around him and merged into the crowd of guests, leaving no direct trail for him to follow.

"Nicole!"

She heard him call her name, his tone adamant, but she didn't stop. She was too afraid if she looked back at Mitch she'd witness the one thing she couldn't bear to see...*his* disappointment in her.

11

MITCH FINISHED his second beer, pushed the empty bottle across the mahogany surface of the bar, and ordered a third from the man serving up drinks for the reception and farewell party. An hour had passed since Nicole had abandoned him, and he still couldn't figure out why she'd deliberately lost that final round. After spending the past week working diligently to win the grand prize her actions contradicted her efforts. Openly giving up was so out of character for her, yet she'd done exactly that.

He'd accepted their award and prize for both of them as she'd requested, but couldn't find the enthusiasm to join in on the festivities. Not without Nicole. And after the way she'd bolted on him, he knew going after her would be futile. Even before forfeiting the contest, she'd spent the day keeping him at arm's length and he knew better than to force his presence on her, or demand answers to the questions preying on his mind.

"Woman troubles?"

Startled by the deep male voice interrupting his thoughts, Mitch glanced toward the sound, at first not recognizing the person who'd spoken to him. The man was standing a few feet away, in the shadows, nursing his own drink. Mitch searched the other man's face, then finally recognized him as C. J. Miller, the resort's pilot. Gone was the cap and aviator glasses he normally wore, and his salt-and-pepper moustache was shaved off. Even his hair was trimmed short and neat, giving him a distinguished look.

He swallowed a long drink of the cold beer the bartender delivered to him, then grinned wryly at C.J. "Are my troubles that obvious?"

C.J. chuckled. "I have to admit, I saw your partner run out on you earlier, and you sitting at the bar isn't a good sign, either."

Mitch lifted a brow toward the other man. "Considering you're holding a drink of your own and keeping yourself inconspicuous, can I assume you've got woman troubles, too?"

"Don't know yet, but I will soon enough." He lifted his glass and swirled the amber contents. "I'd consider this pure liquid courage."

Curious, Mitch asked, "And what to do you need courage for?"

"To finally go after what I've wanted for a very long time, a woman who's been a part of my heart since I first learned what love was all about." He hesitated, his gaze latching on to something or someone in the crowd, and his whole expression softened. "I let her go when I should have fought tooth and nail for her, and now I've been given a second chance to do things the right way, make amends for being such a fool the first time around. Except, after so many years apart, I'm not certain how she'll react."

Mitch followed C.J.'s line of vision, surprised at who'd captured the pilot's attention. "You're sweet on Merrilee?"

"Yeah, I am," the other man admitted, his heart plainly on his sleeve. "I've been avoiding her for the past few weeks, ever since I was hired on as the resort's pilot, but tonight is finally going to be the night of reckoning."

Mitch took another drink of his beer, seeing the uncertainties and hope in C.J.'s eyes, leading him to believe that there was a long history and an interesting story between these two kindred spirits. "I take it you've got a wild fantasy of your own you're hoping to fulfill, huh?"

C.J. nodded. "Yeah, I guess you could say that. But enough about me and *my* woman troubles. Seems to me you could use a bit of advice from an old man who's been around a few times when it comes to women."

Mitch shrugged, figuring he had nowhere pressing to be. "I'm all ears."

"Don't be afraid to lay your feelings on the line and go after what you want," C.J. said, his tone rich with wisdom. "More important, don't let any more time pass than necessary, because it'll just get more difficult to bridge the distance between the two of you."

The man was obviously speaking from his personal experience with Merrilee, but Nicole was a different breed of woman. "The thing is, she's the one putting the distance between us."

"Doesn't look like you're doing much to close it," C.J. refuted, then downed the rest of his drink.

Mitch frowned. "She's stubborn, independent and doesn't like to be told what to do...."

"And you love her," C.J. stated, interrupting his tirade.

As if loving her made any difference at this point. "Yeah, I do."

"Does she know?"

Mitch shook his head. "No." In all honesty, he harbored his own fear—that she'd reject his love.

"Then you've got some talking to do, son. Don't let her go without a fight or you'll regret it for the rest of your life." C.J. set his empty glass on the bar and grinned. "And now, I'm going to go and take my own advice."

Mitch tipped his bottle toward the other man in a salute. "Good luck."

"Same to you." C.J. clapped him on the back in male comradery. "I hope we both get our woman."

Mitch watched the pilot head down the shadowy path, lit by torches, that led toward the resort's main hotel until C.J. disappeared from sight. Needing to find somewhere quiet to ponder what he was going to do about Nicole, Mitch polished off his beer and decided to head down to the beach.

Just as he stood to go, Graham came up to the bar, saw him, and waved him down. "Hey, Mitch, where's Nicole? I've been looking for her and she doesn't seem to be around anywhere."

"She wasn't feeling well and turned in early," he replied, using Nicole's excuse. "I think her wrist was bothering her."

"It's a shame she's missing out on the farewell party." Graham placed his drink order with the bartender and turned back to Mitch. "I was hoping to thank her personally for what she's doing for Penny's brother."

Withdrawing his wallet, Mitch pulled out a few bills and tossed the tip onto the bar's surface while his mind tried to process Graham's odd comment. "Excuse me?"

Graham pushed his glasses up the bridge of his nose with his index finger. "She didn't tell you?"

Mitch had no idea what was going on, but he intended to find out. "Tell me what?"

"She donated her half of her second-place prize money to Penny's brother's trust to help offset the medical bills for his heart transplant."

Mitch felt as though someone had punched him in the gut. "No, I didn't know." And, dammit, why hadn't she told him?

"She's incredible." Graham picked up the drink the bartender slid his way and took a small sip of the tropical concoction. "I don't know many people who'd do something like that for a perfect stranger. You've got yourself quite a woman."

With that statement lingering in the sultry evening air, Graham returned to Penny and the party in progress. Mitch stood there alone, mulling over Graham's comment. Little by little, everything fell into place in his mind, making sense of why she'd deliberately lost the last competition to Penny and Graham—to ensure that Penny won the grand prize money for her brother. And in the process, she'd given up something she'd wanted her whole life—her father's approval.

Stuffing his hands into his shorts pockets, he made his way down to the beach, awed but not at all surprised by Nicole's generosity. Her selfless heart was only one reason he'd fallen in love with her. There were so many vulnerabilities beneath that bravado of hers, and those very human qualities were exactly what made her so special and unique to him. Yet she didn't see herself as loveable, or even worthy. In an attempt to keep from getting hurt emotionally she put on a tough front, but tonight proved just how soft and selfless she truly was.

Finding a lounge chair, he sat down, listening to the waves crash on the shore and watching slivers of moonlight dance on the water. He had no idea how to handle the situation with Nicole, though C.J. had offered some sound advice. But how could he deal with her independent, I-don't-need-anyone-but-myself attitude? He didn't have a clue. All he knew was that he didn't want to do anything to change the woman she was. Yet she obviously believed differently.

Which brought him around to another question: could he live with a woman so intent on depending on no one but herself? He was so used to taking care of everyone around him, and she was incredibly self-sufficient and headstrong. The answer was an unequivocal yes. Yes, he could accept her the way she was if she could just learn to accept herself. And that was something he couldn't control or demand from her. She had to find the strength to believe in him, trust in him, and know that he'd always be there for her—through the good times and bad.

Inhaling a deep breath, he reclined on the chair and stacked his hands behind his head, resisting the urge to go to her. He'd give her until morning to realize for herself that he was a man who'd give her all the acceptance and approval in the world.

And if by then she hadn't come around on her own, he'd just have to convince her to see reason.

NICOLE CHEWED on her thumbnail, her stomach churning in turmoil as she stared at the phone, knowing she couldn't put off the inevitable forever. She had to call her parents and tell them that she'd not only lost the charity event's grand prize, but she'd donated her half of the second-place prize to someone else, as well.

It was her father's reaction she dreaded the most. Disappointment in losing first place. Criticism for giving away the money she'd won. She'd come to expect general disapproval from him, but that didn't make being on the receiving end of his negative comments any easier to bear. But like every other time in her life when she'd been in a similar situation, she'd get past this, too.

Inhaling deeply to calm her internal chaos, she picked up the phone before she lost the nerve and dialed her parent's number. Her mother answered on the second ring with a soft, "Hello?"

She summoned a smile, even though no one was around to see it. "Hi, Mom, it's Nicole."

"Nicole, honey," her mother exclaimed, obviously excited to hear from her. Nicole heard her mother call to her father before addressing her again. "I've been thinking about you and wondering how things are going there on Wild Fantasy. Is the competition over?"

Nicole swallowed the tightness gathering in her throat. "Yes, Mom, it's over." *Thank goodness.*

"Did she win?" her father's voice boomed in the background.

Nicole grimaced, and tamped the familiar sense of failure creeping up on her.

"Hold your horses, Larry," her mother admonished her father, then spoke back into the phone. "How did you and Mitch do?"

"We placed second." Nobody but Mitch ever needed to know that she'd thrown the race, or why. Not her mother, not Penny, not even Merrilee. It was a secret that was hers alone.

"That's fabulous, Nicole!" Her mother's genuine enthusiasm drifted through the phone lines. "Just being one of the top three winners is quite a feat!"

Her mother had no idea just what a feat the charity event had actually been. She and Mitch had been through a lot in the past week—competitions, the wilderness event, her unwillingness to give up even after fracturing her wrist. Compromising. Making love. Swapping stories and discussing deeply emotional issues. She'd never shared so much with another man in such a short period of time.

"There's something else I need to tell you," she said, and quickly went on before she chickened out. "I donated my half of the second-place prize to another charity."

"Oh," was her mother's initial, stunned reply.

Nicole squeezed her eyes shut, swearing she wouldn't let insecurities get the best of her or steal away the sense of pride she'd felt when she'd lost the race to Penny. "The money is going to a very good cause," she explained, wrapping the phone cord around her fingers. "It's for an eighteen-year-old boy who needs a heart transplant, and the money is going into a trust for his surgery and medical bills. His sister is here on the island, and she was trying to win the charity event for him. She won first place, but I know that won't be enough money to cover the expenses ahead of him—"

"Honey," her mother interrupted gently. "I'll admit you threw me off guard a minute ago, but what you did was very commendable. That prize money was yours to do what you thought was best, and I completely support your decision. There'll be other charity events for my organization, but only one chance for this boy. I'm very proud of you."

The tears she'd valiantly tried holding back finally spilled free when she realized what her mother had just given her—praise for a good deed and unconditional support. "Thank you, Mom, for understanding," she whispered. And that was enough for her.

"What has Nicole done this time?" Larry asked from somewhere behind her mother.

Nicole ignored her father's voice with more ease than in the past. She didn't need to talk to her father. Not because his opinion didn't matter to her, but because she was proud of herself at last. She was no longer a little girl who needed her father's blessing, but an adult woman who already had the support of a good man. The best man. Mitch.

Nicole settled back on the couch, curled her legs beneath her and wiped away the moisture on her cheeks. She spent the next half hour talking to her mother about the weeklong events, the fun she'd had, what a good sport Mitch had been, and how she'd fractured her wrist. It was one of the easiest, most enjoyable conversations she'd had with her mother in a long time, without any expectations hanging over Nicole or her feeling as though she had to prove her worth.

By the time she hung up the phone, Nicole felt higher than a kite and had a whole new outlook on her life and her future. Her time on the island forced her to realize just how important it was that she be true to herself, and she had Mitch to thank for being the person to give her the courage to face that truth.

Maybe winning this charity event is something you need

to do for nobody but yourself, he'd said, and she'd done exactly that, and reaped the wonderful sense of pride and respect that came with being her own person. She refused to allow her father to be the barometer of how she judged herself any longer, she thought, lifting her chin defiantly. Only she had the right to judge herself and her actions, and she was unequivocally satisfied with the decision she'd made tonight.

The only thing she regretted was doubting Mitch and his belief in her. He was a man who knew all her insecurities and vulnerabilities and even her worst habits, and he accepted her without reservation, and without asking or expecting her to change. She'd been the one who'd thought she'd have to live up to certain expectations to please him, and feared she'd fall short. Yet he'd never demanded anything more from her than she'd been able to give. In return, he was protective, caring, but never overpowering and controlling. The man believed in equality, and he was the best thing that had ever walked into her life.

She jumped up from the couch and headed out of her cottage and back toward the farewell party. She needed to talk to Mitch, to tell him that she loved him and to convince him that she was willing to take the biggest risk of her life...and wanted him along for the wild and crazy ride.

But Mitch was no longer at the reception, and no one seemed to know where he'd gone. She returned to her place and called his room, but there was no answer. All she could do was leave a voice mail message asking him to call her when he returned.

Her phone never rang. Sometime after midnight she crawled into bed with her heart heavy with doubts and uncertainties. She'd come so far on this trip, but she wondered if she'd end up just as she'd been before this vacation—alone and lonely.

IT HAD BEEN a very long day but Merrilee finally bid good-night to Danielle after wrapping up the farewell party. Then she headed toward the bank of elevators that would take her to her suite.

The final competition had been exciting, and she'd been pleased to present the winners with their awards and prizes. Overall, the week had been a tremendous success, with many partners working together to bring out personal strengths and overcome weaknesses. There had been a few intimate, romantic connections between couples, and plenty of fantasies fulfilled as well, which was always a nice way to end the event.

She pressed the up button and waited for the elevator to arrive, hoping that things worked out between Mitch and Nicole. She'd noticed a change between them when they'd returned from the wilderness event, and the tension had still been evident during the question-and-answer session. And it most definitely had not been a good sign when Nicole had left the reception immediately following the last competition.

At first Merrilee had thought Nicole's disappearing act had been because of her injury, but then she'd observed Mitch at the farewell party and recognized the signs of a man who was torn over a woman. Something was keeping them apart, and while she had the strong urge to play mediator and give them a happily ever after of their own, she knew this was a fantasy only the two of them could fulfill. But she was a strong believer in fate, and if things were meant to be between Mitch and Nicole, they'd find a way to bridge the distance and work out their differences.

The elevator doors slid open quietly, and Merrilee stepped inside the lift and finally let her own personal disappointment settle in. Fate definitely hadn't been on *her* side tonight. She'd spent the day battling an underlying current of anticipation, certain she'd finally meet up with C.J. at the farewell party, only to have her hopes deflated when he'd been a no-show.

She shouldn't have been surprised that he'd stood her up. He'd been skirting her for weeks now, and she was beginning to think the man was an illusionist, maybe even a figment of her imagination.

While it was too late to do anything tonight about her pilot ignoring a direct summons, tomorrow first thing she'd demand his presence in her office and maybe even hand him his termination papers for insubordination, she thought, knowing she was letting her frustration get the best of her. She was honest enough to admit to herself that professional annoyance wasn't the main reason behind her disappointment. It was more personal.

She still had his book of Shakespeare's poems to return, poems she treasured as she'd begun a nightly ritual of curling up in bed with C.J.'s leather-bound volume. Reading a few of those romantic sonnets each evening brought back so many wonderful memories of her beloved Charlie and filled that gaping loneliness within her she'd lived with for so long. And so she'd wanted to meet *him* tonight—the man, not the pilot—because he'd brought back memories of Charlie and given her a surreal hope for the future. A hope he'd dashed when he'd broken his promise and hadn't shown up at the farewell reception.

The elevator pinged its arrival at the top floor of the hotel and she stepped out and walked down the long, silent corridor to her suite. She breathed in the surprising scent of roses and frowned. Now her mind was playing tricks on her, making her imagine something that wasn't even there. Her fingers absently touched the ruby heart pendant she hadn't taken off since she'd received the gift from her secret admirer, who'd yet to make his identity known. She shook her head. Between C.J. avoiding her, her elusive admirer, and all the memories of Charlie swamping her lately she was beginning to think that maybe *she* needed a vacation.

She laughed at her silliness, withdrew her key card from the pocket of her slacks and opened her door. The interior of her suite was as dark as she'd left it that afternoon, and again the fragrant rush of roses greeted her, stronger this time, making her dizzy from the potent scent.

Confused and startled, she flipped the light switch on and gasped in shock as she took in her surroundings. Her entire entryway and what she could see of her living room were filled with dozens and dozens of ruby-red roses. Literally hundreds of them covered every bare space available. Even the carpet was covered with vibrant, velvet petals.

Not sure what to think, she tentatively walked inside and came to an abrupt stop when she saw a man sitting in a chair in the living room. A man who looked like C.J., but without his cap, glasses and moustache. A man who also possessed an uncanny resemblance to her memories of Charlie. It was his eyes that held her spellbound—a pure, clear blue that seemed to see straight to her soul.

He smiled and gestured to the floral display. "Because they're your favorite," he said, his voice low and rich and hauntingly familiar.

She shook her head hard, but he remained sitting there. He had to be a dream. A ghost. An apparition. Any and all would apply, because there was no possible way this moment could be real. "C.J...Charlie?" She heard the confusion in her tight voice, felt the room spin around her. Somehow, someway, she managed to hang on to her composure.

He started to stand, and she held out a hand to stop him. "Stay right where you are," she demanded fiercely, thankful that he obeyed her command, at least until she got to the bottom of his visit. "Who are you?"

His gaze held hers, steady and true. "C. J. Miller... and Charlie Miller."

Oh, God. How did he know about Charlie? Furious at the idea of someone playing games with her, she straightened indignantly. "If this is some kind of cruel trick—"

"This is no trick, Merrie," he promised, calling her by the name only Charlie had ever used for her. "It's me. Charlie."

Denial rose swiftly within her, choking her with anger and disbelief. "But that's impossible! Charlie died in the war over thirty years ago!"

"Yes, a part of him did die in the war," he stated, his gentle gaze never leaving her face. "But the best part of him lived...the part that never stopped loving you."

A crushing pressure clamped down on her chest, right near the vicinity of her heart, and aching tears of illogical hope gathered in her throat. She wanted to believe him, and couldn't deny the familiar traits that three decades hadn't changed. Yet none of this made sense when she'd lived her whole adult life with the knowledge that she'd lost her one true love.

So many questions whirled in her head, but all she could manage to ask was, "How... Why?"

Those two words encompassed the whole spectrum of what she needed to know, and he instinctively understood. He started from the beginning, and she stood there across the room from him, unable to move, listening to Charlie tell her about the horrors of war, his desperate move to save his own life, and his time as a prisoner of war. Of how he'd returned to find she'd married Oliver, and believed it was for the best that he not interfere in her life or come between her relationship with her new husband. He told her about marrying Evelyn, all about his two girls whom he adored, and how he'd never stopped thinking about her, loving her. After his wife died he'd discovered that she was a widow, too, and that she'd started her chain of fantasy resorts.

He'd hired on as her pilot to get close to her, sent her all those gifts as a secret admirer to rekindle memories, including the leather-bound volume of Shakespeare's poems and sonnets. It was the original book she'd given him so many years ago, which had kept him going through some of his darkest hours. The dedication page, she learned, had been ripped out by a vindictive guard. All of his gifts, and every move he'd made on the island for the past few weeks, were an attempt to pursue her to see what, if anything, was still between them.

But it was obvious to Merrilee that time and distance hadn't diluted their love for each other. If anything, their devotion had strengthened and grown rich and replete by deep, abiding memories. Charlie had been, and always would be, her one and only true love. Her soul mate. And he was here, now, still wanting her in return.

The enormity of everything that had just transpired swept her away, and she buried her face in her hands and gave into the emotional release. Her whole body shook as she cried for all they'd lost. Her tears of sadness were gradually replaced with tears of joy for the second chance they'd been given.

She felt his arms encircle her, familiar and strong, and this time she didn't deny either one of them. She sank against him, clinging to him like she would never let go. Indeed, she didn't ever want to let him go for fear that this was all a wonderful dream. But his touch was reassuring, the heat of his body real.

"I'm so, so sorry, Merrie," he murmured, stroking his hand down her back, soothing the tremors still vibrating through her. "I never, ever meant to hurt you. If I could go back in time and do everything differently I would. But there's one thing that's remained true and will never change, and that's my love for you."

She pulled back to look up at him, seeing the sincerity in his blue eyes, and spoke the words she never thought she'd have the opportunity to say again. "I love you, too, Charlie."

He lowered his head and kissed her, and it was as if they'd never been apart. Their embrace encompassed tenderness, passion and desire. It was all still there, along with an intimate connection that had transcended time and their years apart.

The kiss ended, but he kept her close, so that their heartbeats echoed as one. "You know, I've really become fond of this fantasy business of yours. In fact, I've got a knack for relating to your guests," he said with a slightly cocky grin. "And I'm hoping like hell you'll keep me on."

She laughed, feeling like the light, carefree girl he'd known in their youth. "A few hours ago I was ready to fire you."

His eyes twinkled flirtatiously. "You forget how irresistible I can be."

"It's coming back to me very quickly, and I'm sure I can be swayed to keep you around."

His teasing expression grew serious. "I know this might be very presumptuous of me, but I want a future with you, Merrie. I want to be a part of your life, permanently. I want what we were denied so many years ago."

She searched his handsome features, so afraid to hope. "Just what are you saying?"

He let her go, and she immediately missed his warmth. "I swear I'm going to do it right this time around." Nervous laughter escaped him as he withdrew a small black velvet jewelers' box from his pants pocket. "I bought this ring the day I returned home from the war, before I knew you'd married Oliver, and I never took it back. I've dreamed of this moment, of putting this ring on your finger and making you mine. Forever."

He opened the box, revealing a bridal set with a dozen dazzling diamonds set in white gold. The ring was a timeless, classic style, and back then must have cost Charlie a small fortune.

He went down on one knee in front of her, grabbed her left hand, and stared deeply into her eyes. "Merrilee

Schaefer, will you do me the honor of marrying me and being my wife? Of growing old with me, and letting me be the one to grant your fondest wishes and deepest desires?''

She smiled, realizing in that moment that she was surrounded by all her favorite things...roses, rubies, poems and Charlie. Especially Charlie. He made everything complete for her. "Oh, yes," she breathed, nearly bursting with happiness.

And in that once-in-a-lifetime moment, as her one and only love slipped an engagement ring on her finger, Merrilee's greatest fantasy was fulfilled.

HE COULDN'T WAIT any longer. After spending the night down at the beach mulling over his relationship with Nicole, at the break of dawn Mitch headed to Nicole's cottage to make good on C.J.'s advice. He was going after what he wanted and not letting any more time pass between him and Nicole than necessary. Having been on the receiving end of Nicole's obstinate attitude, he knew if he waited for her to come around on her own it would take her an eternity. And he didn't have an eternity, not when they were due to leave the island that afternoon and their future was at stake.

He intended to lay his feelings on the line and tell her that he loved her. No beating around the bush. And after that, if she chose to ignore her own emotions and return to Colorado separately from him, then at least she'd do so feeling as miserable as he.

Satisfied with his plan, he knocked on her door, loudly and repeatedly, until he heard her sleepy voice mutter from the other side, "I'm coming, I'm coming."

The door opened with her trying to give the sash on

her silky robe one last tug to secure the lapels, and she winced as the fingers of her injured hand weren't quite as coordinated as the other. Her hands stilled and her slumberous eyes widened in surprise when she saw it was him. "Mitch—"

Before she could tell him to leave, or slam the door in his face, he brushed past her into the cottage.

She followed him inside, frowning as she gave him a quick once-over. "Where have you been? You look like hell."

He barked out a laugh, though he could find no real amusement in her statement when he felt as though the rest of his life depended on the outcome of their confrontation. "I spent the night on a lounge chair on the beach." He'd gone back to his room to use the bathroom and brush his teeth, but hadn't wasted time to shower, shave or change. Pacing to the far side of the living room, he spun around to face her again. "We need to talk, and not only will I not take no for an answer, I'm not leaving until we get a few things settled."

Her expression turned wary, and uncertainties glimmered in her eyes. But she didn't deny him. "Okay."

Her easy assent when he'd been anticipating a fight or argument took him off guard for a moment. He was feeling aggressive, acting assertive, which was so *not* like him. And here was Nicole, more calm and poised than he'd ever seen her.

He braced his hands on his hips, and kept his mind on his purpose for being there. "First of all, I know why you threw the last competition."

She looked visibly startled, but quickly recovered. "You do?"

He nodded brusquely and pinned her with his gaze.

"Graham came up to me after you left the reception and told me he wanted to thank you for donating your half of the second-place prize money to Penny's brother's trust."

She tucked a sleep-tousled strand of honey-blond hair behind her ear, though her gaze remained cautious. "Yes, that's true," she said softly.

"And then I started thinking why you'd deliberately answer the last question wrong when you knew our answers would match." Slowly, he approached her, stopping two feet away. "You did it for Penny, didn't you? So she'd win the first-place prize for her brother."

Her spine straightened, and her chin raised a few notches. "Yes. She needed the money more than we did."

He bit back a smile, grateful to see a glimmer of that stubborn, independent woman he loved. "I most certainly agree. And by throwing the competition, you gave up the possibility of gaining your father's approval."

She looked away, focusing her attention somewhere beyond his shoulder. "It wasn't something I thought about at the time."

No, but he was sure she'd thought about it since, and wondered if she'd regretted her spur-of-the-moment actions. With a tender touch, he redirected her gaze back to his. "Why didn't you tell me why you lost to Penny, instead of running off like you did?"

"I was scared." Her reply was honest, baring deep vulnerabilities that grabbed at his heart.

His thumb caressed the smooth line of her jaw. "Of what?"

She swallowed hard and admitted, "I couldn't bear to see your disappointment in me."

He dropped his hand, blew out a breath, and shook his head in disbelief. "If you've learned anything at all about me this week, sweetheart, you'd know that you could never disappoint me. Frustrate me, irritate me, make me want to shake some sense into you sometimes...but never disappointment."

She bit her bottom lip and whispered, "I know."

It was an answer he hadn't expected. An argument from her, yes. Her acquiescence, no. Confusion assailed him. "And how do you know that about me now when you didn't believe it last night?"

She stepped around him and opened the living room curtains, then the glass slider leading to her deck, letting the morning warmth and sunshine pour into the room. She stared out toward the ocean and was quiet for so long he almost thought she wasn't going to answer him.

"I spoke to my mother last night," she finally said, her tone steady and unwavering.

He remained still and quiet behind her, listening, wanting to hear it all. Suspecting, too, this is where he'd find out about her father's reaction.

"I heard my father in the background asking if I'd won, and I got this huge knot in my stomach because I knew I was going to have to tell him that not only did I lose, but I gave away my second-place prize money, as well. All those same insecurities came flooding back..." Her voice trailed off, and she turned back around to face him, the fingers of her good hand threading through the sash on her robe. "So, I told my mother everything, and of course she was stunned that I donated the money to another charity. But then, you know what?"

"What?" he said, even though he knew she was going to tell him anyway.

"She told me that she supported my decision. And in my heart I knew you would, too. And suddenly it no longer mattered to me what my father thought. *I* felt so good about what I'd done for Penny, I didn't need my father's praise to validate a decision I'd made from the heart." The smile curving her lips made her positively glow. "I'm not the same person I was when I first stepped onto this island a week ago, and I'm glad of that. Now, I'm going home with something far more rewarding and important than my father's approval."

He sensed the change in her, a softness and emotional fortitude that radiated from the inside out. "And what's that?"

"For all the things I've accomplished in my life, I finally feel proud of *me*. And I have you to thank for giving me the courage to accept myself for who and what I am, win or lose."

He raised his brows in surprise. "You do?"

She nodded and glided toward him, the front of her robe fluttering open to give him a glimpse of a smooth, tanned thigh and silky panties. "You told me that winning isn't everything. That sometimes losing can bring great things, too." Smiling, she captured his stubbled cheeks between her one good palm and her casted one and stared deeply into his eyes. "Losing did bring great things for me. Peace of mind. Respect. And the strength to admit that I'm good enough for you, with no expectations. And the greatest thing of all is loving you, Mitchell Lassiter."

"Aw, dammit," he muttered, and feigned a boyish pout. "I wanted to say it first!"

She tossed her head back and laughed, the sound light and carefree and joyful. "You honest to goodness love me?"

"After everything we've shared this week, how could you not know?" He settled his hands on her waist, and his fingers caressed cool silk, making him anxious to stroke more heated flesh. "As strange as it sounds, despite the chaos I know I'm in for, I can't imagine my life without you in it."

"Are you sure you're going to be able to put up with me?" she asked sassily. "I know I've got a smart mouth sometimes—"

He lifted a brow. *"Sometimes?"*

"And I can be a bit bossy—"

Laughter sputtered out of him. "A *bit?*"

"And I'm a little headstrong and stubborn—"

He rolled his eyes heavenward. "A *little?*"

She made a face at him. "You know all my faults."

"Yeah, I do," he said huskily. "And I love you anyway."

"And I know yours."

He frowned. "I didn't know I had any."

A smile quirked the corner of her mouth. "It's that responsible, respectable, stuffy thing that you've got going."

He sighed and drew her hips closer to his until their lower bodies meshed. "Then I guess I'm just going to have to depend on you to make sure I get enough adventure in my life."

"Hmm, I think I can arrange a few adventures with All Seasons," she said thoughtfully, wickedly, making him wonder what she had planned for him. "Yeah, I think we'll complement one another quite nicely."

He had no doubt of that. Swinging her up into his arms, he headed down the short hallway to the bedroom.

She gasped and clung to his shoulders. "What are you doing?"

"What I've been dying to do since we returned from our wilderness survival event. I'm going to make love to you on a nice, soft, comfortable bed." Gently, he deposited her on the rumpled sheets and followed her down, careful of her wrist as he settled in next to her. He untied the sash on her robe and spread the sides open, revealing a silky camisole and matching panties. "We've got a few more hours before our love-slave fantasy is over, and I have a few more sexy scenarios in mind I'd like to try out if you're game."

"Oh, most definitely," she purred, and moaned when he slipped his hand beneath the hem of her camisole and pushed it up over her breasts.

His mouth latched on to a puckered nipple, suckling and laving the crest, and she sighed in pure pleasure. "I wish we didn't have to leave the island," she said breathlessly. "Not yet, anyway."

He lifted his head and stared into her eyes, feeling spontaneous and daring. "Then let's stay."

With one hand, she tugged his T-shirt upward, and he stripped it off for her. Her fingers fluttered over his chest and down to his belly. "That's a lovely idea, but we can't stay."

"And why not?" He didn't give her a chance to answer as he pulled off her top and panties, then worked on the rest of his clothes until they were both naked.

"You said you can't do much at work with your fractured wrist, and I'm feeling rebellious enough to call and tell my brother to handle things for another week." It still amazed him how comfortable he was with the thought when he'd spent so many years trying to be everyone's caretaker. Now it was time to take care of him and his needs, and it started and ended with this incredible woman who was his.

"Another week?" she asked, her voice rising incredulously, despite the excitement in her eyes. "My, you *are* feeling defiant."

"Yeah, I am." He grinned, satisfied that he was able to enjoy himself so much. And then he planted a quick kiss on her lips that melded into a slow, heated, passionate embrace that nearly sent them both over the edge. He pulled back, his heart thudding hard in his chest as he gazed down at her. Unbridled sensuality etched her features, and love shone bright in her eyes, and that's all he needed to see to confirm he was about to do the right thing.

He threaded his fingers through her soft hair and eased a thigh between hers to get closer. "Want to do something completely reckless and impulsive and shock everyone back home?"

"You know you don't have to ask me something like that twice," she said with sexy amusement. "What did you have in mind?"

"Marry me, Nicole," he said, his voice deep and strong and certain. "Here on Wild Fantasy."

She blinked, stunned at his declaration. "You can't be serious."

"Oh, but I am." Picking up her right hand, he pressed her palm on his chest, right over his heart. "It feels right and undeniable, here in my heart. I've always felt something for you, and it took this week to realize I was half in love with you the past few years. Now I'm completely in love with you, and time isn't going to change how I feel, and nothing you could do could make me love you any less."

Tears of happiness pooled in her eyes. "You're crazy."

"Yeah, maybe I am." He swiped away a tear that trickled from the corner of her eye. "I'd bungee jump from the highest bridge in the world for you. I'd sky dive from the heavens for you. I'd—"

She covered his mouth with her hand, laughing at the outrageous ways he'd prove his love for her. "How can I refuse? Yes, I'll marry you. Here on Wild Fantasy, and as soon as possible." She crooked her finger at him as anticipation flushed across her skin. "Now come here and make good on your earlier promise, slave."

"Yes, Mistress." Grinning sinfully, he grabbed the sash from her robe and wove the strip of silk through his fingers suggestively, his erotic intent making her eager and undeniably aroused.

And as they made love, heart, body and soul, Mitch knew spending a lifetime with Nicole would prove to be the wildest fantasy of all.

_____Epilogue_____

One week later

"BY THE POWER vested in me, I now pronounce both couples husband and wife." The minister who'd performed the private ceremony smiled at the newlyweds standing beneath an arch of vibrant red roses, baby's breath and lush green fern. "Charlie Miller and Mitch Lassiter, you may kiss your brides."

Nicole turned to her husband, overwhelmed with love for this man who'd made her life so complete she couldn't imagine living another day without him in it. She lifted her lips as he lowered his head, accepting a kiss that was brimming with tenderness and devotion and promised her decades of passion, loyalty and love.

Applause broke out behind them from the intimate gathering of guests who'd shared in their special day. With a satisfied sigh, Mitch rested his forehead against hers and smiled. "I guess now I have to share you with our parents, huh?"

She laughed, recognizing the sexy gleam in his rich brown eyes. "Just for a little while, Mitchell. I still can't get over that you got them here for our wedding. And Merrilee did an amazing job putting together such a beautiful, elegant reception for all of us."

Nicole was still touched and awed at the story Merrilee had shared with them about C.J. being Charlie.

When Mitch had requested getting married on Wild Fantasy, Nicole had suggested a double ceremony between the four of them. Considering Merrilee and Charlie were just as anxious to become husband and wife and start their new lives together, it all seemed to work out for the best.

She placed another quick kiss on Mitch's lips. "A few dances, a little dinner, a couple of bites of cake, and then we'll slip away for our honeymoon night."

With that promise, they turned and headed hand in hand down the red velvet runner toward their parents, who'd been flown in as a surprise by Mitch to witness the double ceremony. Hugs and well-wishes were accepted by two ecstatic mothers who couldn't have been happier that their eldest children had fallen in love with each other. Then Nicole turned to her father who had a warm smile on his face, and a bit of moisture in his eyes so unlike the man she'd known her entire life.

He gathered her into his embrace, careful of her casted arm, and kissed her cheek. "You look absolutely beautiful."

In that moment, Nicole was glad that her father had been there to share in her day. She no longer needed his approval, but getting married was a once-in-a-lifetime celebration that belonged to both families. As always, Mitch knew exactly what she needed without her saying a word. "Thank you, Dad."

Larry reached out to Mitch and shook his hand. "Take care of my girl, Lassiter," he said gruffly.

"Yes, sir." Mitch draped his arm across Nicole's shoulder, holding her close to his side. "What do you say you and I go and congratulate Charlie and Merrilee?"

Nicole nodded her agreement, and they left their parents for a moment to head across the lawn to the woman who'd had her own fantasy fulfilled today. Mitch leaned close and whispered in Nicole's ear, "I think your father is mellowing a bit."

"Hmm," she replied, knowing that her father still had a long way to go in coming around with her, but his being there today was a huge step. "I think he's happy that I've settled down at last like a woman should. And I think it helps that he likes you. Give him a grandbaby and he might soften up a bit more."

Mitch arched a dark brow her way. "Is that a challenge I hear in your voice, wife?"

"It's most definitely an invitation to start practicing, as much and as often as possible," she said with a sassy grin, then spoke of the two times they'd made love without protection. "And who knows? There might already be a baby on the way."

"Are you okay with that?"

His voice was gentle and concerned, and her heart swelled with an abundance of love for this man who understood her so well. "With you by my side, I'm *more* than okay with that."

From the other side of the landscaped lawn with a view overlooking the ocean, Merrilee watched Mitch and Nicole approach her and Charlie. She smiled, thinking that Nicole looked as radiant as she herself felt. And the incredible man standing beside Merrilee was responsible for her transformation.

Charlie had insisted on having his two girls there for the wedding, along with their families, and the warm reception Merrilee had felt upon meeting his family made everything in her life come full circle. The little cherub of a granddaughter she held in her arms was Charlie's by blood, but was now hers as well by marriage. He also had a precocious little four-year-old grandson who was excited to learn that he had a new grandma. She'd never been able to have kids of her own, and now finally had babies to spoil. And she was loving every minute of spontaneous hugs and being the center of a four-year-old's constant chatter.

Merrilee handed the baby girl back to her mother so she could congratulate Nicole and Mitch and give them each a hug. "Thank you so much for allowing me and Charlie to share in your day."

"We wouldn't have it any other way." Nicole and Mitch exchanged a loving look. "You've given us a wonderful fantasy with this wedding and reception, and we're thrilled that the two of you are a part of it."

Charlie lifted Merrilee's hand to his lips and brushed a kiss across the back of her knuckles. "And from here on, *I'll* be fulfilling any fantasies she might get a hankering for."

Merrilee blushed, but managed a grin for her guests. "Why do I get the feeling that I've got my hands full with this man?"

Charlie winked at her. "I've got a lot of lost time to make up for, sweetheart."

She laughed, as did Mitch and Nicole. There was no denying that Charlie was absolutely perfect for her. And for her business. With her four flourishing island resorts, the two of them had many more fantasies ahead of them to fulfill for their guests. And as Nicole and Mitch had proved, and others before them, there was love to be found even in the most unlikely places.

Harlequin truly does
make any time special. . . .
This year we are celebrating
weddings in style!

A
Walk
Down
the Aisle
WEDDING CELEBRATION

To help us celebrate, we want you to tell us how wearing the Harlequin wedding gown will make your wedding day special. As the grand prize, Harlequin will offer one lucky bride the chance to **"Walk Down the Aisle"** in the Harlequin wedding gown!

There's more...

For her honeymoon, she and her groom will spend five nights at the **Hyatt Regency Maui.** As part of this five-night honeymoon at the hotel renowned for its romantic attractions, the couple will enjoy a candlelit dinner for two in Swan Court, a sunset sail on the hotel's catamaran, and duet spa treatments.

A HYATT RESORT AND SPA   Maui • Molokai • Lanai

To enter, please write, in, 250 words or less, how wearing the Harlequin wedding gown will make your wedding day special. The entry will be judged based on its emotionally compelling nature, its originality and creativity, and its sincerity. This contest is open to Canadian and U.S. residents only and to those who are 18 years of age and older. There is no purchase necessary to enter. Void where prohibited. See further contest rules attached. Please send your entry to:

Walk Down the Aisle Contest

In Canada	In U.S.A.
P.O. Box 637	P.O. Box 9076
Fort Erie, Ontario	3010 Walden Ave.
L2A 5X3	Buffalo, NY 14269-9076

You can also enter by visiting www.eHarlequin.com
Win the Harlequin wedding gown and the vacation of a lifetime!
The deadline for entries is October 1, 2001.

HARLEQUIN®
Makes any time special ®

PHWDACONT1

HARLEQUIN WALK DOWN THE AISLE TO MAUI CONTEST 1197
OFFICIAL RULES
NO PURCHASE NECESSARY TO ENTER

1. To enter, follow directions published in the offer to which you are responding. Contest begins April 2, 2001, and ends on October 1, 2001. Method of entry may vary. Mailed entries must be postmarked by October 1, 2001, and received by October 8, 2001.

2. Contest entry may be, at times, presented via the Internet, but will be restricted solely to residents of certain georgraphic areas that are disclosed on the Web site. To enter via the Internet, if permissible, access the Harlequin Web site (www.eHarlequin.com) and follow the directions displayed online. Online entries must be received by 11:59 p.m. E.S.T. on October 1, 2001.

   In lieu of submitting an entry online, enter by mail by hand-printing (or typing) on an 8½" x 11" plain piece of paper, your name, address (including zip code), Contest number/name and in 250 words or fewer, why winning a Harlequin wedding dress would make your wedding day special. Mail via first-class mail to: Harlequin Walk Down the Aisle Contest 1197, (in the U.S.) P.O. Box 9076, 3010 Walden Avenue, Buffalo, NY 14269-9076, (in Canada) P.O. Box 637, Fort Erie, Ontario L2A 5X3, Canada.

   Limit one entry per person, household address and e-mail address. Online and/or mailed entries received from persons residing in geographic areas in which Internet entry is not permissible will be disqualified.

3. Contests will be judged by a panel of members of the Harlequin editorial, marketing and public relations staff based on the following criteria:

   - Originality and Creativity—50%
   - Emotionally Compelling—25%
   - Sincerity—25%

   In the event of a tie, duplicate prizes will be awarded. Decisions of the judges are final.

4. All entries become the property of Torstar Corp. and will not be returned. No responsibility is assumed for lost, late, illegible, incomplete, inaccurate, nondelivered or misdirected mail or misdirected e-mail, for technical, hardware or software failures of any kind, lost or unavailable network connections, or failed, incomplete, garbled or delayed computer transmission or any human error which may occur in the receipt or processing of the entries in this Contest.

5. Contest open only to residents of the U.S. (except Puerto Rico) and Canada, who are 18 years of age or older, and is void wherever prohibited by law; all applicable laws and regulations apply. Any litigation within the Province of Quebec respecting the conduct or organization of a publicity contest may be submitted to the Régie des alcools, des courses et des jeux for a ruling. Any litigation respecting the awarding of a prize may be submitted to the Régie des alcools, des courses et des jeux only for the purpose of helping the parties reach a settlement. Employees and immediate family members of Torstar Corp. and D. L. Blair, Inc., their affiliates, subsidiaries and all other agencies, entities and persons connected with the use, marketing or conduct of this Contest are not eligible to enter. Taxes on prizes are the sole responsibility of winners. Acceptance of any prize offered constitutes permission to use winner's name, photograph or other likeness for the purposes of advertising, trade and promotion on behalf of Torstar Corp., its affiliates and subsidiaries without further compensation to the winner, unless prohibited by law.

6. Winners will be determined no later than November 15, 2001, and will be notified by mail. Winners will be required to sign and return an Affidavit of Eligibility form within 15 days after winner notification. Noncompliance within that time period may result in disqualification and an alternative winner may be selected. Winners of trip must execute a Release of Liability prior to ticketing and must possess required travel documents (e.g. passport, photo ID) where applicable. Trip must be completed by November 2002. No substitution of prize permitted by winner. Torstar Corp. and D. L. Blair, Inc., their parents, affiliates, and subsidiaries are not responsible for errors in printing or electronic presentation of Contest, entries and/or game pieces. In the event of printing or other errors which may result in unintended prize values or duplication of prizes, all affected game pieces or entries shall be null and void. If for any reason the Internet portion of the Contest is not capable of running as planned, including infection by computer virus, bugs, tampering, unauthorized intervention, fraud, technical failures, or any other causes beyond the control of Torstar Corp. which corrupt or affect the administration, secrecy, fairness, integrity or proper conduct of the Contest, Torstar Corp. reserves the right, at its sole discretion, to disqualify any individual who tampers with the entry process and to cancel, terminate, modify or suspend the Contest or the Internet portion thereof. In the event of a dispute regarding an online entry, the entry will be deemed submitted by the authorized holder of the e-mail account submitted at the time of entry. Authorized account holder is defined as the natural person who is assigned to an e-mail address by an Internet access provider, online service provider or other organization that is responsible for arranging e-mail address for the domain associated with the submitted e-mail address. **Purchase or acceptance of a product offer does not improve your chances of winning.**

7. Prizes: (1) Grand Prize—A Harlequin wedding dress (approximate retail value: $3,500) and a 5-night/6-day honeymoon trip to Maui, HI, including round-trip air transportation provided by Maui Visitors Bureau from Los Angeles International Airport (winner is responsible for transportation to and from Los Angeles International Airport) and a Harlequin Romance Package, including hotel accomodations (double occupancy) at the Hyatt Regency Maui Resort and Spa, dinner for (2) two at Swan Court, a sunset sail on Kiele V and a spa treatment for the winner (approximate retail value: $4,000); (5) Five runner-up prizes of a $1000 gift certificate to selected retail outlets to be determined by Sponsor (retail value $1000 ea.). Prizes consist of only those items listed as part of the prize. Limit one prize per person. All prizes are valued in U.S. currency.

8. For a list of winners (available after December 17, 2001) send a self-addressed, stamped envelope to: Harlequin Walk Down the Aisle Contest 1197 Winners, P.O. Box 4200 Blair, NE 68009-4200 or you may access the www.eHarlequin.com Web site through January 15, 2002.

Contest sponsored by Torstar Corp., P.O. Box 9042, Buffalo, NY 14269-9042, U.S.A.

PHWDACONT2

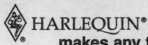